FX NOZAKHERE

DuSable City

THE UNDERSIDE OF CHICAGO

FX NOZAKHERE

DuSable City
DUSABLE CITY: The Underside of Chicago

Copyright © 2019 **Marc J. Hart**

BlaqRayn Publishing
134 Andrew Drive
Reidsville NC, 27320

To the best of said publisher's knowledge, this is an original manuscript and is the sole property of author **FX NOZAKHERE** (Marc J. Hart)

Printed in the United States of America
ISBN: 9781692614935

Printed by **KDP 2019**
Published by **BlaqRayn Publishing Plus 2019**

DEDICATION

This work of fiction is dedicated to the Indigenous Sauk Natives who went to war with the settlers.

To the Potowatami, Miami, Illiniwek, Kikapoo, Shawnee, Iroquois, Fox, Ottawa and all other natives who inhabited this land now called Illinois and Chicago.

*To **Jean Baptiste Pointe DuSable**, the first settler of Chicago.*

To Ida B. Wells, Emmit Till, Nahaz Rogers, Steve Cokely, Harold Washington and Black-hawk.

INTRODUCTION

You're finally on a date with THE ONE, the person of your dreams! How do you feel? What goes through your mind as you reminisce on your loving late grandfather? What do you say to your baby right before you leave them for a long time? What do you talk about when you're hanging out with your oldest church going friends? What memories appear in your minds' eye while attending your childhood church or even celebrating an anniversary with your loved one?

Do you remember the good times, being a silly kid with your buddies hanging out past the time when the street lights came on? What romantic interludes do you remember while doing adventurous activities with your significant other? What feels better than getting well after a bout with illness?

Maybe it's being an inspiration to the people you serve? We can reflect on these feelings and thoughts while taking the simple pleasure of a quiet night drive home from a hard day at work, or simply being at home with the family. These are questions of a highly emotional gravitas. It is these thoughts and feelings that contribute to our experiences. They are what makes us, us.

All of these human experiences are happening within this rather peculiar city named Chicago. Positioned between New York and Los Angeles, it towers over the mid-west, casting at times an ominous shadow. A city wide fire could not destroy it, yet wars with the Sauk Natives almost prevented it from ever existing. It is home to some of the worst political corruption known in American history. Yet, one of the most tragic turning points in this city's history was the murder of one of its native sons in the south, a crime that accelerated the Civil Rights Movement.

Today Chicago will make news for a murder, perhaps in the Wild Hundreds. The corrupt mayor cutting a ribbon at a gentrified Black neighborhood or a fifty degree day in the middle of July. But, what will not make the news are the stories within these pages. Peek into the world of real life people as they experience their full selves within this city founded by a Haitian man named Jean Baptiste Pointe DuSable, this peculiar city named Chicago.

DuSable City

THE UNDERSIDE OF CHICAGO

FX NOZAKHERE

MIDNIGHT MASS

It's the last few minutes of December 24th and I'm walking up the steps of my old Catholic grammar school for the late night church service to bring in Christmas. Even though I've come to midnight service here before, it never ceases to amaze me how a lot of things about the church and school are different now. Our Lady of Peace is now Winnie Mandela Academy, the church now caters to Haitians with mass done in Creole.

Being here always brings back memories, the smell of candle wax burning, the reverberations of sound in the great hall, the beautiful artwork on the stained glass windows. As I scan the church, I can remember something in every square foot. Every young face of my classmates flashes in my mind and I can name almost all of them. I take a deep breath, yes, lots of memories here, both good and bad.

The church itself is still beautiful, despite my non-belief that keeps me at a distance. I am again amazed at how the building has withstood time and the new features added since I was a student here.

For the past several years I've attended the Christmas Eve, twelve am service for old times sake, and each time I sit in the back so as to not disrupt the ceremony. And, each time I come here I am visited by a little boy. He's always here, he always seeks me out just to say "hi" for he knows I'm always here on this particular night.

I put his age at about six, he has on glasses around a big head crowned with an uneven afro. He is wearing clothes that would be considered nerdy, with his wrinkled tiny brown slacks and clean white button up shirt tucked into his pants. A cute little boy that walks up to my pew, looks at me then flashes a crooked smile. I melt a little and scoot over to let him sit down next to me.

"Hi little man," I greet him. He responds with a soft "hi" with his shy self. We smile at each other and turn our attention to the priest conducting mass.

During the Patois driven mass, I turn to the child and

jokingly whisper, "Do you understand what he's saying?"

He smiles, turns to me, fidgets and replies "No but I can feel what he's saying." Strange.

Strange child, rather profound I think to myself, but I soon start to understand what he means as I could tell what part of the mass was taking place. The portion of the ceremony comes where people get up to get their host and wine. I turn to the boy, asking..

"Are you going up to get some?"

"No." he replies smiling, "Are you?"

"No, but I'm going to buy my own body of Christ wafers."

"That's a good idea, but where you gonna' buy them from? The priest?" He replied with a grin.

We both laughed loud enough that it reverberated to the people a few rows over, they turned to look at me. I put my hand over my mouth, with a surprised look on my face.

"Uh oh, sorry." I looked down at the child who was doing

the same while holding back a laugh. We connected with two childish giggles.

He turned his attention to the altar but I held my gaze on him for a few seconds more. I looked around to see if any adult may be looking for him or if anyone even remotely looked like he could be theirs. Everybody in the sanctuary kept among themselves with their respective people.

"Where's your mommy and daddy?" I asked and before I could draw another breath he answered, "At home."

"So, who are you here with?" I asked, looking again at the crowd to see if I'd missed someone like a grandparent.

He replied without looking up at me, "I came here with you."

"What?" I thought to myself, I shot a look down at him.

"I always do. I always come here with you." His voice was so innocent and timid. He looked up at me but this time there was no smile. He then looked slowly back to the altar proceedings.

I stared down at him; this adorable little boy, legs

swinging off the pew, hands fidgeting, big eyes behind big glasses

blinking. That's when I notice something. I looked closer, the

hairs on the nape of my neck standing at attention. This kid

wasn't breathing! Instead of sniffles, a tiny clearing of the throat,

a small abdomen or chest moving, there was nothing.

As soon as I noticed this, I heard a wheeze emanate from

him. It started out small, almost unnoticeable, then it became

louder and more coarse. Yet, there was still no up-and-down

movement in his chest, indicative of breaths taken.

"Is that...you? Are you having trouble breathing?" I

nervously ask. I look down at his fidgeting hands that were now

still.

Suddenly dark, red blood dripped, quickly forming a

puddle in his small hands. The blood overflowed onto his lap,

staining his church clothes. I turned my undivided attention on

him, raising my voice.

"Hey what's wrong? Where's that coming from?" I asked,

pointing to the still flowing blood that was beginning to pool on the floor beneath his feet. He didn't move at all. The wheezing grew louder, harder, while terror and panic coursed through me.

Is this child going to die right in front of me, was my thought, as I grabbed his hand to both comfort him and to see where the blood was coming from. Praying to something divine that someone in this cathedral would see what was happening and come help.

I held his hands, his blood now spilling onto me but I didn't care. I moved his hands away from his body; it was his stomach, the blood was coming from his abdomen.

I quickly start to wipe away blood and examine him. All the while, he just sat there calmly, barely moving. I frantically looked up at the people around us; surely someone was witnessing this? No one seemed to be paying any attention to us, but how was that possible, considering the amount of blood this child was losing and the not so quiet commotion I was making.

Just as panic starts to take over, the child looks up at me, pleading in a jagged voice..

"Don't let me die." Electric fear shot through me like lightning. My mouth hung open and my body froze.

"What?!"

Blood begins pouring from the child's abdomen like water from a faucet, forming mini-rivers on the floor. His white button up shirt now a bright crimson. The blood made splattering noises on the church floor, accompanied by the ever louder wheezing. I'm in a state of quiet hysteria, what do I fucking do?!

The child suddenly stands, seemingly unaffected by the wheezing and blood. I freeze, looking at him. He turns to walk out the row, but now he's limping badly. Turning to me, he repeated ominously. "Don't let me die." I'm horrified, as I stare into his eyes, still frozen in panic.

Yet somehow, the calmness of the child enabled me to collect myself just long enough to think clearly. *This child is familiar,* I realized, as I stared into the little boy's face. As if he'd read my thoughts, he replied promptly.

"There's nothing but the dead here...take me with you.

Please don't leave me here." There were no more cute smiles, no more soft child's voice. The now harsh, labored and congested voice reverberated in my head. Those big, sad, watering eyes pierced my soul.

I began to breathe long drawn out breaths, not believing what I heard my own lips say, "Yes....I'll take you with me."

His smile returned, he touched my hand with his bloody one and excitedly skipped back to the church foyer. I stood up slowly, looking around to see if anybody saw anything. Not one head turned, not one person noticed us. I looked toward the foyer for the little boy but he was gone. Just as he had disappeared, the blood vanished from my hand, the pew and the floor.

As I started down the isle, I felt a sudden heaviness in my chest, my shoulders hunched slightly and I felt a light wheeze in my breathing. As suddenly as it came, it went, not enough to really concern me. I continued walking towards the entrance of the church, still looking for this peculiar little boy.

Upon entering the foyer, I felt a pain shoot through my

stomach. I grabbed my abdomen only to notice scaly skin and open sores now spreading onto my hand. I anguished at the mere thought of what was happening to me; the asthma, the skin disease, the stomach ulcers, all of them were returning at once. Was everything an illusion? The church? The child? Is this my time to die? Revisited by old demons? Hunched over, I slowly walk to the doors of the church. *I need air, I need to breathe, I don't want this pain again!*

I managed enough strength to push open the large wooden church doors; the change in air bringing with it clear breathing almost immediately. I didn't even mind the twenty seven degree temperature. The pain in my stomach slowly subsided and my mind screamed, *my hands, what of my hands?*

Even before I looked at them, I could feel normalcy returning...yes, elasticity in my skin again. A wave of relief rushed through my body and with it a feeling of remorse lined with hope. Remorse was for the part of me that felt as if I was wilting on a vine and yet now there was hope for a complete restoration.

DuSableCity

I walked away from the sadness of what was in my past and, with the child and all its innocent hope awakened in me, I bravely headed into the darkness of what I will be in my future. Leaving the old man behind and carrying the child with me into the night.

THE PEOPLE'S CANDIDATE

There was applause and praise.

"...Reverend Williams asked me something long ago, just as I was getting started in politics...he asked me one question. One question to test whether or not I was worthy to represent you today. That question was 'do you love Black people?' Without taking a breath, I immediately answered 'yes I do'! I love my people! And, if Chicago as a whole, wants to go forward into the next century, then those of us left out, those of us forgotten, the so-called permanent underclass, a majority of which is made up of African American people, will need to be at the forefront of change in this city. Change for an equitable access to wealth, jobs, health care! We cannot wait for this too long. We've been buried under the quagmire of corruption, false promises and kept in check by rogue police long enough and I'm saying, NO MORE! NO DAMN MORE!!!"

The crowd in the church lavished praise upon her, they

loved her, they supported her, they voted for her. She was the first really serious African American woman candidate for Chicago Mayor. The others before her were either too weak a candidate or, as many in this very church speculated, ran campaigns to disrupt other genuine campaigns. Not her, her sincerity resonated with the people. A people tired of the monotonous litany of liars and corrupt politicians. She was not selling lofty, abstract, feel-good verbalizations. She relayed real world solutions to the police accountability issues, the city debt, food deserts, drug hot spots and the rent being too damn high.

One aspect of her appeal was that Angelique Baron was a strikingly beautiful woman. A statuesque five foot ten inch tall political whirlwind, dressed in business attire, standard red button up long sleeve blouse and matching red knee length skirt. Most men would not dare admit that her lighter skin, long jet black hair and shapely body were a huge part of garnering their attention but *it was* her political expertise that garnered their respect and their vote.

Initial shallowness aside, Angelique Baron was highly

adept in civics and well informed on the nature of Chicago politics, being the daughter of a powerful former South-side Alderwoman, Angelique Baron, the senior. Coming from political royalty, it would seem she was destined to continue her family's political vision.

She soaked in the praise and standing ovation but she wouldn't let it go to her head. Amid the church inspired clamor, she raised her hand, closed her eyes for a second to take in the energy of the crowd and waved as she stepped away from the podium. A smiling Pastor Williams, in his flowing purple church robe, rose to greet her with a hug. He had known her since she was a little girl and his pride in her showed when he looked at her.

He moved towards the microphone, "Angelique Baron ladies and gentlemen, brothers and sisters, let the church say amen and hallelujah!!! This is the leadership we need! This is the leadership the people deserve!" His amplified voice was barely audible over the ovation.

Angelique went down the line, shaking the hands of the figures behind the podium. Church deacons, aldermen and other candidates aspiring to various positions. Pastor Williams was already introducing the next speaker by the time Angelique stepped down from the stage off to the right. She stopped to shake a few people's hands from the audience who wanted to have their brush with what they hoped would be the future mayor. A smile, a handshake, a hug, then she made her way through a side door into the stairwell, a tall thin dark skinned man in a dark suit followed closely behind her.

A look of seriousness erupted on her face and her brow furrowed as she took in the audience with her security detail, "Any news?"

"Not much yet...." before the man could finish, Pastor Williams innocently interrupted.

"They love you young lady, I love you! The lawd loves ya." His smiling face switched to one of a serious countenance. "You got a minute..."

"Of course Pastor."

"...Before you go?" Pastor Williams added. Angelique

Baron nodded her head slightly to her detail, he returned the nod, exiting the stairwell.

"That meeting…" Pastor Williams' face immediately took on a worried and stern look, "…it didn't go well. I don't think things will fall the way we need them to." The Pastor's arms folded, her arms folded; this was a debriefing between two whom were as close as family but swam in complex political waters.

The background noise of the speaker at the podium and the crowd's reaction permeated the stairwell, forcing them to go deeper into the stairwell for closer contact in order to hear above the raucous without the need to shout.

"It was O'Shea wasn't it?" Angelique asked.

"Of course." Pastor Williams replied.

"Ok, I can talk with him. He's not really a difficult, unreasonable man…he will negotiate." Angelique reassured her lifelong spiritual mentor with a smile and a pat on the shoulder.

"I hope so, because you know what may happen when this group goes forward with this…Angelique, we need those contracts…" Williams reminded her.

Angelique politely cut him off, her hand still on his shoulder, "I know, but really he's not….I don't think he's married to the ideas they're putting forth…"

"Ok…" The Pastor didn't sound too reassured.

"…I'll talk with him. I'm on good terms with him so I'm sure he will negotiate with me." She hoped her further assurances would put him at ease.

"Surprisingly, that man….huh." Shaking his head, Williams released a sigh of relief at this woman he'd known since she was a little girl. As far as he was concerned she was always honest and decorous with him. He trusted his spiritual niece, as he jokingly referred to her when she was growing up.

Angelique smiled, walked towards the door, opening it to find her driver in the pews. When her eyes caught him, he was already looking in her direction. She made a twirling motion with her hand, signaling for him to get the car. He nodded, rising to follow her order. Angelique smiled at her spiritual uncle and gave him a child's hug.

"Don't worry Unc, I'll see what I can do. I know how important this is to you and others.." She said, as she hugged her Pastor. They moved out of the embrace, walking through the door and back into the rally. Pastor Williams returned to his hosting duties, while Angelique made her way to the back of the church to leave, only slowing down long enough to shake hands and wave.

Another small gathering of admirers and voters in the church foyer delayed her exit from the church. She didn't mind at all, she met with every one of them, eagerly shaking hands and flashing her warm genuine smile. She was a political firebrand but the people were also attracted to her sweetheart demeanor; they felt her sincerity and hung their hopes on it. It was the hope for a politician that would give the people the attention, fair play and integrity they sorely missed in others.

Finally, the door of the church swung open and Angelique, with her briefcase, purse and jacket in hand, floated out and directly into the awaiting vehicle.

DuSable City

With a smile she looked at the well dressed, dark suited Black man, "Thank you very much," and carefully entered the backseat. The driver closed the door and hurriedly made his way to the drivers' side. Once in, he was ready to take his passenger where she needed to go.

"I really don't need a crowd with me tonight Roy. I just want to go home, decompress and relax. No crowds tonight, we clear?"

"Crystal ma'am." Roy responded politely. The engine in the Black Cadillac SUV hums as they pull away from the church, heading towards her home.

It was finally quiet, save the hum of the engine. Her ears were ringing just a little from the songs, the applause and the shouting. Angelique greeted a lot of people, listened to a lot of views, a lot of complaints, analysis and praise. She appreciated it all but she needed a respite from it before she went forward with the rest of her night. She slumped slightly in her seat, something her iconic mother would correct her for.

FX NOZAKHERE

"Barons don't slump Angelique Jr..Sit up!" Her mother's voice reverberated in her mind. All the standards required for an upper class girl were not wasted on Angelique Baron II as she was formally called. The second in the family after her mother, who named her, to hold the name Angelique Baron. Family and friends just called her AJ or Angie Jr, but as she began to follow her mother into politics, she'd had to use her full formal name.

For a while, it was odd for people to get used to a woman as a junior but her prospects in filling the shoes of a beloved political figure, her mother, dispelled any awkwardness. Now, little AJ was sitting in the back of a luxury SUV being chauffeured around the city as she runs for the mayoral office, a move from the aldermen seat her mother once held. The ballet lessons, piano lessons, Jack and Jill, sweet sixteen coming out party; it all got on her nerves when she was coming up, but it had all paid off.

It was nine twenty three pm. The SUV merged onto the Eisenhower Expressway and maneuvered into the left lane. To the left, the Chicago downtown skyline caught her eye. It was the majestic sight of a beautiful metropolis topped with purple lights adorning the dual antennae of **The Sears Tower**. Her mind focused on what was crawling within that beauty; expensive whores and their greedy puppeteers all protected by a gun slinging gang of barely literate brutes. She rode through the old post office property, a gigantic waste of empty space. A building so large an expressway flowed right through it.

Coming from under the cover of the edifice, the SUV traveled through downtown Chicago and past the milieu of homeless people shuffling about, making their way to Pacific Gardens Mission to get a bed for the night or a comfortable spot on the sidewalk to collapse and sleep until morning.

Angelique kept her eyes in the direction of Lake Michigan when the SUV turned onto Lake Shore Drive. She searched for the distant lights of the inlet crib a few miles from the shore. A strange structure out in Lake Michigan she learned about long ago when her grammar school friend told her about her grandfather working on it. Her eyes located it, barely visible lights blinking on and off, signaling its' presence in the dark. She thought of the manpower and the time it took to construct this vital part of Chicago's infrastructure in the 1920's. She also thought of where Black people were during that time, wondering how many, if any Black men, had worked on such an effort.

The SUV hit a soft curve which brought in view the Hyde Park Building in which Harold Washington lived. Angelique leaned over slightly to get a better look at the former residence of Chicago's first African American Mayor. Along with those thoughts of pride, were her speculations on the circumstances surrounding his death. *Very peculiar,* she thought to herself, as she kept eye contact with the building as the SUV passed it on it's way further south.

The end of Lake Shore Drive comes abruptly, the SUV passed grassy fields, ordered rocks lining a beautiful shoreline and world famous museums. It ended with two gas stations and a man selling fruit in the middle of the street among gang members, elderly drug addicts strewn about the sidewalks and college students coming home from night classes. She was now easing down Jeffery Boulevard and with that, memories of people trying to change the name of this street to Malcolm X Boulevard. She remembered that and the effort years later to change the name of Lake Shore Drive to DuSable Drive. Both efforts failed due to the obstruction of the mostly white city council and their reach into city departments to block those and future efforts of historic recognition. Angelique shook her head slightly at the passing memories.

Finally, the SUV pulled into the driveway of Angelique's home in the affluent Pill Hill. "It's ok Roy, I'm good from here, you don't have to walk me in." she said softly.

She quickly gathered her suitcase, purse and jacket. Right as she pulled the handle on the door, she paused and looked toward her home for half a second then swung open the door and stepped out the car. She surveyed the surrounding area, Friday night, it was eleven minutes after ten at night, the streets of Pill Hill were quiet save an occasional car passing through.

With an emotionless stare, she walked around the car and up the walkway to her front door. The driver slowly started to back out, not wanting to leave her defenseless as she worked the lock on the door. He finally drove off after watching her enter her home, closing the door behind her.

Once inside the dark foyer, her silhouette placed her briefcase and purse on a table to the right of the door. On the left, she carefully hung her jacket on a leaning coat rack. She slowly turned to lock the top lock, then the middle, then the bottom, very carefully.

Her footsteps echoed from the foyer, through the living room, past the stairs that led to the upper level of the house and into the kitchen. Not turning on any light, she caressed the handle of the refrigerator and gently pulled it open. The pale light from the fridge illuminated a small section of the kitchen, interrupted only with her body. She leaned backwards just a bit to get a better view of the contents. Her eyes swept pass eggs, butter, raw cows milk, rows of neatly arranged vegetables and roots; edamame, broccoli, carrots, and celery, all stored in Tupperware. Finally, she reached in and grabbed an energy drink.

"It may be a long night of work ahead..." she spoke softly to herself, thinking the caffeine will keep the energy flowing.

DuSable City

Quietly, slowly she closes the door, not making a sound. The light from the fridge is wiped away by the door closing, as her figure walks out the dark kitchen, the sound of a can being popped open pierces the quiet stillness.

On her way to the living room, she stops at a desk in the hallway, she doesn't turn to it. Without looking, she touches the handle on the drawer with her left hand, draws her finger across the metal then grips the handle with her index finger, reaching in and pulling out a knife. It's black handled, marked with West Afrikaan tribal symbols; the blade, a wide six inch grooved piece of menacing steel. She dangles it in her hand as her arm drops to her side. She takes a sip of the cold energy drink as she makes her way through the darkness, past a lamp she doesn't bother to turn on.

Walking to a stop in front of a glass cabinet, she places her drink on the top of the entertainment center and pulls the glass door open to reveal a setup of several components. She raises the knife to press the power switch on the CD player, then slowly moves the knife down to the disc selector. She presses it and the rumble of a rotating disc tray emanates from underneath the machinery; it stops. Still using the knife, she presses the play button. There's a barely audible whirring sound from the inside of the disc player. Then, the soft sound of horns, violins, and a slow, rhythmic beat commences. She closed her eyes and shakes her head as if a powerful testimony is about to start.

"You touch me baaabe....buuuut doooon't cha' know you can't hiiiide.....no no baaaaby...." The unmistakable baritone voice of Barry White fills the air. She moves her body in rhythm and turns up the volume.

Arms raised, head tilted down, eyes closed, mouth open to form lyrics while her butt grinds in a serpentine cadence. She dances, backwards, slowly, never missing a beat, never stumbling over a piece of furniture; she knows her house well. Taking another gulp of her energy drink, she winds her body slowly back towards the kitchen. She stops.

White continued to sing "Playing yo' game baaaby......yo' gaaaame baaaby.....just yooouuu aaaand meee........" as she dipped deeper, mouthing the lyrics, face winced, arms outstretched; in her right hand an energy drink, in her left, a knife. "Playing yo' game baaaby......yo' gaaaame baaayby.........nooobody but yyyyoooooooouuuuuu and meeee!".

She danced over to the door at the back of the kitchen then paused, she was entranced by the music. She held her head up towards the ceiling, this time a slight smile finally came across her red lips. She stood there, slightly gyrating to the rhythm, the knife now dangling between her thumb and index finger. She took the last gulp of the energy drink and placed it on the counter before her. She took a breath, as if sighing because she had to leave the music.

Gripping the door handle, she abruptly opened the door where a dim light diffused into the kitchen. She stepped in and one step down, turned and slowly closed the door behind her.

Her steps punctuated her intentions and a faint whimper emanated from the dark basement. Using the knife to flick a switch, Angelique stood as a towering silhouette among a now well lit area. A timid breath was heard just above the music coming from upstairs. She stared hard in front of her, just standing in that position for a few seconds. There was another soft whimper. She looked to her right at a table containing a box of salt, a feather, a set of needles, a screw driver, a hammer and a pair of pliers. All these items lay in order on a white and red spotted towel. She reached for none of these. Instead, she grabbed the chair pushed under the table.

Turning to re-establish her penance stare, she loudly dragged the chair several feet. The grinding steel against the jagged concrete of the unfinished basement floor caused more nervous whimpers and a murmur. She stopped, turned the chair around and sat in the seat, leaning back. She hiked up her skirt high enough to show much of her thick brown thigh wrapped in silk, the knife in full view, now firmly gripped in her hand.

"Now Mr. O'Shea, where were we?" She stared into the eyes of her prey.

In front of her, whimpering and sweating, both scared and inexplicably relieved, was an older, red-faced white man, his hands and ankles tied up with duct tape. A red ball had been stuffed in his mouth and secured by more tape. Bits of dried blood clung to his gray hair and forehead. He wore stained, unzipped suit pants and a white t-shirt soaked with sweat.

"Ah yes, our....negotiations." Their eyes met. There were tears in his, fire in hers.

The relief he'd felt instantly evaporated as her right hand cupped her breast and flicked her nipple beneath her red blouse; she then raised the knife, sliding it across her tongue. Upstairs, Barry White continued to serenade the basement business. "Playing yo' game baaaybe...yo'gaaaame baaaybe...nooobody but yyyyooooooouuuuuu and meeee!"

Deep within the night, barely audible, a man screamed ....then begged for more.

A LONG WALK

This is the happiest I've ever been in my life! I still cannot believe I am presently with the woman of my dreams, right now! I'm actually here, with her! Ok, I'm spazzing out and I can't let her notice my excitement. She might think I'm some type of creep and get scared off. Keep it cool, just relax.

It's a perfect night, perfect seventy degree weather under a perfect cloudless starry sky. Despite the light pollution of the Chicago downtown skyline, the stars are still oddly extra bright. I didn't pay much attention to it because all my attention was on her. The woman I've been enchanted with for months and in those months, I've tried tirelessly to ask her out.

"I thought it was cute," she said to me one day about how I constantly tried to get her attention, like some love struck school boy. It was one of the first running jokes we shared which was a relief to me. I wanted to connect with her on something and if that something was me sometimes making a fool of myself to get with her, then so be it…it was worth it. Her smile was worth it. My spirits lifted every time I'd catch her taking a quick look at me and then turn away smiling.

Our slow walk down the Magnificent Mile, occasionally brought us into accidental contact with each other; it was my nerves. As much as I tried not to seem nervous, I'd get goofy and clumsy. She had that affect on me.

I'm conscious of my jacket collar being folded down, my jeans not being crumpled at my boots, my afro being evenly groomed, hoping my all black wasn't making her wonder in anyway. Praying my very casual attire complimented her immaculate white button up blouse, earth brown wrinkle free slacks and curly, exploding afro. This woman wore everything well, I mean, nothing looked bad on her. She had a wonderful shape; her crowning beauty being her big brown eyes.

"You want to get a frozen yogurt...uhhh, it's right down here," I asked with my stammering ass. She let out a little laugh as if she notices my nervousness.

"I can't. it's too late to eat that. It's the sugar." Dammit! I had to remember this sistah is a fitness expert. I should know better!

"I should know better than to suggest that shit at 10pm, my bad." I had to try to smooth over that slight faux pas.

"No, it's cool. In fact, since it's getting late, usually I'd be making my way home to get to bed..."

Oh shit...

"...But, I think I much rather be here taking in this vibe." WHEW! Man, I thought I was fuckin' up! She'd rather be here.. great! That makes me feel so good! Dammit! She doesn't know how her saying that and her smiling at me is electrifying my whole spirit right now! I'm freaking out over here!

"Oh cool, glad you feel that way." Calm, cool and collected was the way to go.

As we approach the Michigan Avenue bridge, where the sidewalk thins, a line of tourists flood toward us. I immediately step in front of her so as to not allow anyone to bump into her. I lead us through the human maze, occasionally looking back to make sure I wasn't too far ahead of her. We smile at each other, silently sharing the inside joke concerning the influx of picture taking visitors to Chicago.

Finally reaching the other side of the bridge, unofficially North Michigan Avenue, I gently place my fingertips on her shoulders and maneuver to her right. I had to take my gentleman place nearest the curb. That should win me some more points.

"You know, I never understood what that meant. Why men have to walk nearest the curb? Where did that come from?" she said with a smirk.

Fuck, well there goes that idea.

"You know, I'm not sure either. I think it had something to do with prostitution or..." She interjected with raised eyebrows.

"Prostitution? Oh, so I'm a ho?" I could hear the smile in her words but I was too nervous to recognize it.

"No, No! NO! I meant..." She starts laughing, I think she knows I'm nervous and is playing with me.

"So what does it mean Captain Save-A Ho?" She winks at

me and laughs in earnest.

"OOOHH! So you got jokes!" Humor is so damn sexy.

She chuckled, placing her hand on my arm. "I remember a brother long ago telling me that a man walking on the street side of the woman meant protection." I was genuinely confused.

"Protection from what?" I asked honestly.

"Like if a vehicle or whatever splashed water on the sidewalk driving by, or if a car lost control and jumped the curb…" she explained.

"Oh, so I'm supposed to get muddy water splashed on me or…I have to catch a car to protect you?! And I'm supposed to just be ok with that?"

"Damn straight!" she quickly answered with smiling conviction. "No excuses neither! Get your ass curbside and start catching cars homie! Protect the Black woman!" she yelled.

"I will! I will! But I think you're well qualified to defend me too. It's not like you sit at home on the couch eating pie all day." I couldn't help but check out her square shoulder frame, thick muscular thighs and a gluteus muscle that signified she knew and understood squats. Just one of the many things I found attractive about her; she took care of herself.

"I can and *would* if I needed to." She replied.

"Awwww, you'd protect me?" I wasn't being patronizing. I was truly surprised and touched by her words.

"Well, first it's your job as a man, right? I mean, ok, I take kick boxing, lift weights but it's no big deal really." She was simultaneously shy and bragging as she expressed her position.

"Ahh, I see…'Do not turn your face towards people and do not walk through the world exhaltantly. The Most High does not like one that is self deluded and boastful..'" I strained to remember the line.

"Hmm?" She turned to me and watched my lips move as I recited the lines. "What is that? It sounded poetic."

"It's from the Quran. Sura 31 something I think, verse 16, 17 or 18…can't remember." My eyes met hers and I couldn't look away despite my nervousness.

"You Moslem?" she inquired innocently. Before I could answer, she interjected, "wait, is it Moslem or Muslim? I never was sure."

"It's Muslim, with a strong u sound, and yeah, I used to be Muslim."

She watched me talk with a smirk as if impressed with my menial words. Or at least I hoped she was impressed. I told her my time in the Nation of Islam and hoping that their militancy wouldn't give her apprehension about me. After all it was two years ago.

"Used to be? So why did you leave Islam?" she asked. As we walked, I told her about my time in the organization, the captains I met, the MGT's, except the one I dated; the training, the studying and eventually my doubts. Doubts in the doctrine that led me to ask questions, tough questions, questions that landed me in bad standing and in private meetings with the FOI Captain.

"After that, I just kind of tendered my resignation and

left." I was still holding a little regret from that experience. She notices and shows a bit of concern on her beautiful, dark brown face.

We're slowly walking past the Wrigley Building, a beautiful edifice of white brick further illuminated by ground level lights, all of which are a sharp contrast to the night sky. A night sky that now has two very bright stars near each other. I hadn't noticed them before.

"That Quran verse you quoted?" She interrupted my silent observation with her beautiful voice.

"Yes."

"It kind of reminds me of a verse in the Book of Revelation, Chapter 3 verse 17. See how I knew the whole chapter and verse? Heathen."

"HAHAA!!! Did you just call me a heathen?" Again, her humor…I loved it. "But do you remember the whole verse? I did."

She gives me the "really" look.

"Well, almost all of it." I added.

"Umphhh! Yeah ok. 'Because thou sayest I am rich and have increased with goods and I have no need for nothing, and knowest not that thou art wretched' I love that word by the way, 'and miserable…" her voice morphs into a mocking preacher tone, "…and poora and bliiiiiind and nekkid!"

"Nekkid?" I asked, a bit confounded.

"Nekkid." she replied.

I suddenly felt a few drops of water on my face. Despite staying focused on our conversation, I realize we're far away from the Chicago River under the bridge we just walked over. I look up.

"What's up?" She looks at me then looks up, following my lead.

"I just felt some water drop on my face. Maybe it was a few drops of rain but…"

"I don't see any clouds." She interjected. "It might be from the top of the building, some moisture on the roof carried by the wind."

"Yeah, that's probably it." I replied, wiping my forehead and still a little perplexed.

As my finger wiped over my left eye, I glimpsed the night sky again. There I noticed a third star, much brighter than the first two. *A helicopter*, I reasoned in my mind, *the other two were probably helicopters as well or maybe planes.*

A white tissue came towards my cheek, it was her, wiping off the remainder of the water drops. She dabbed my cheek carefully and softly, it felt so good that something so small would garner her attention to me. I felt like gold.

"Humility." She said softly.

"What about it?" I asked, still enraptured by her caress on my cheek.

"The scriptures…the Quran scripture you quoted and the Bible one I quoted. I feel like they are communicating to us to be humble in all ways." Her hands, still holding the tissue, are now moving with her words. "The material things of this world, that's not really us, they're not what define us. What ultimately defines us is..."

We say it simultaneously "...our actions," we laugh at the same time.

She continues, "Right! Our deeds, especially our deeds towards those who are the most vulnerable, the ones that are struggling."

I can't give her my full attention because another sprinkle of water hits my face. Now I'm getting a little irritated but I can't show her that.

"Where is this water coming from?"

"You got splashed again?" She asks, as she folds the tissue in half to wipe off the new drops but now my attention is drawn away due to the sudden dizziness I feel.

"Wait, hold up..." My head becomes light as the street begins a subtle wobble.

"You ok?! What's wrong? Come sit down over here." She took my arm and led me to a stone bench on the sidewalk. We walked slowly and the closer I got to the bench, the further away it seemed. By the time I finally sat down, my head was swimming. This was strange.

She immediately goes into doctor mode, "You feel dizzy? Lightheaded? What did you eat today? What can I do?" Her doctor mode is accompanied with a dose of worry, I can hear it in her voice. I have to let her know I'm alright, calm her down.

"Yeah I...I feel better already. I guess I just needed to sit down for a minute."

"It's ok. You need any water or anything?" She's still holding my arm; that alone is making me feel better.

"Besides the mystery water that keeps landing on my face, I think I'm good..." I smile, she smiles despite the situation. I then pause to check myself, "...yeah, I'm better now. I guess I didn't eat enough, plus the excitement of the night must have taken a slight toll on me."

"I get the not eating part but the excitement?" she responded.

I take a breath and muster up the courage to blurt it out. "The excitement of being here with you, of course." I say it as if she should know that already.

She smiles but there's concern on her face, "Oh, that's sweet, but I don't want you getting sick on me. If you want, I can drive when we leave." *She's concerned about me*! Yes! After all the anxiety, the worry about whether or not a woman of this caliber would even look in my direction. After all that, *she's* concerned about *me*. She cares. Our eyes meet. We stare just for a few seconds, it felt like an hour.

I clear my throat to break the spell. "I'm feeling better now." My words relax her a bit but she keeps her hand around my arm as I start to rise to my feet.

"I think it's time to get moving." I declared.

She smiled and said "Ok, lets get you home to rest." The lights in the sky are even brighter now, I notice as I get to my feet.

"Oh, I'm not si..." A sharp pain engulfs my chest and abdomen. I heave forward. What is going on?! Immediately nausea strikes and rushes my throat. A liquid ejects violently from my mouth, it's red and I almost choke. What is happening?!

"OH MY GOD, IS THAT BLOOD?! SIT BACK DOWN!" she screams, as more blood pours from my mouth and nose. I gag, trying to catch my breath! I stumble back to the stone bench as another gush of red ejects from my mouth. Between that and the pain, I somehow notice the vomit spews out then back towards my face, but I'm sitting with my head pointed to the ground.

"Turn his head!" The pain is violent! Unimaginable! I cannot take it much more!

"Get towels now! Clean his face!"

What? A another voice? From where? I can feel her grabbing my shoulders, she's screaming but I can't hear her voice!

"We need another dose now!" Through the pain, I can see people walking fast past me, ignoring my plight. The buildings start to smear and blur into the night sky, diluting it. I can hear voices but I can't hear hers anymore. Where's her voice?! WHY

FX NOZAKHERE
CAN'T I HEAR HER?!

"How the hell did this happen?!"

"We have a situation, get in here!" Where are these voices coming from? I look up but the vomit covering my face clouds my vision. I can only turn my head as the rest of my body appears to have stopped moving. I notice the lights, three before but now there are six. As each light grew larger, I wondered *are they landing*? Where is the beautiful and perfect night sky? It's gone! She's gone! I can feel my insides being pulled out!

"He's waking up!" Figures frantically rush about the table, a man hurriedly rushes to measure a syringe.

"I have it ready now!" On the table, a body flails, pulling the tubes connected to it. An arm breaks free from a restraint and viciously yanks the breathing mask from his face. He screams.

"What's...AAAHHKKK...happening?! Where is she?!" Two orderlies immediately grab the man, pushing his shoulders down.

"Mr...we need you...we need you to relax. We're going to

put you back under! Can you hear me?!

Hold him down! Stop him from moving!" Another voice

orders.

Two women, petite but strong, help restrain the panicked

man on the table, another nurse moves quickly to the arm with the

most tubes in it. He finds the IV, pushing the syringe contents into

the tube. "Ok, it's in…we have a window of time for that

Isoflurane, but hurry up!"

His movements on the table slowed. His arms, which were

tensed, slowly begin the progression to relaxation. His eyes, wide

open, start to dim and close.

"What the fuck happened? How much is in there?!"

"We had the proper amount, based on his information. I

don't understand his reaction." The voices mix, some agitated,

others calm in relief. The pain in the patients' body slowly starts

to numb. With the last bit of waking energy and coherence, the

man on the table slightly lifts his head to figure out what is

transpiring. A gaze towards torso reveals his abdomen ripped open, dark blood surrounding the flesh canyon and dripping onto the floor. He screams but the contents on the syringe only allow him a silent scream.

From the gaping maw that was his abdomen, he sees blood drenched intestines hanging over his side, scissors stabbed straight down into the hole. Two large scalpels appear to be stuck in his side, all of it surrounded by bloody towels and gauze. His head drops back down on the table just in time for a nurse to place the mask on his mouth. The gas enters the mask and seeps down into his lungs but the pain is not going away.

What seems like a lifetime passes and the man on the table has not reached unconsciousness. A feeling of panic overcomes him as the numbness begins to fade away and the sharp, agonizing pain returns completely.

Unfamiliar faces stare down at him, all with puzzled looks. His eyes wide open, scan the room for some sign, something that can take him away from this waking nightmare; he's looking for her face. The pain is constant in his entire body, he is a terrified witness to his own measured disembowelment. He cannot go under, he cannot sleep, he cannot stop thinking of her in the midst

of his agony. His face freezes with terror, realizing…

There are four hours left to this surgery.

WHILE MAKING LOVE A RIOT BROKE OUT

"GET DOWN! GET FUCKING DOWN!!!"

"STOP! STOP!!! YOU'RE KILLING HIM..HE'S BLEEDING!!!"

Lasan was frantic, caught in a turbine of chaos. Bodies pushing from every direction and falling all around him; everything was a blur. He was running as fast as he could through a maze of screaming humans.

"MOVE BACK I SAID!!!"

"AAAAAAHHHHHH!!!"

He tried to focus his eyes and ears for a familiar sight and sound, a voice that could draw him to her. A fist missed it's intended target and caught Lasan on the back of his head. He jerked forward but he didn't lose focus. A body slammed into him with a police helmet tumbling off.

"I FUCKING SAID MOVE BACK!!!"

Lasan fought through, pushing bodies, fortifying his legs so that he wouldn't fall. His mind was as fast as his heart and as fast as his feet would allow him to move.

"ANYA!!" he yelled in a cracked accent, hoping to hear her familiar voice in the chaos.

"ANYAAAA!!!" he cried louder, a look of desperation overcoming his red Celtic face, as the sound of his voice bounced off the wall of violent humanity around him.

"FUCK YOU, FUCKING PIG!!!" was the only clear voice he heard.

Denying that wall, Lasan pushed through, trying to get to the other side. His body was rocked left and right, shoved violently and kicked, a liquid splashed from somewhere and sprinkled his face. He turned his head quickly then refocused. He saw an opening, it was small and temporary. He started towards it and jumped through only to be caught by the waist when it collapsed. He pushed and elbowed against the bodies that closed in on him, a long forgotten struggle with claustrophobia was quickly remembered. He tried not to think about it, getting to Anya preoccupied his mind.

The opening he'd fought so hard for was large enough to offer him a glancing survey of the entire situation. A situation that turned from a peaceful demonstration to one of bloodshed within minutes. They had gathered to protest the unjust murder of an unarmed African American woman by the police. There had been others but this one was significant due to the fact that the murder victim was an activist. So strong had her voice been against the injustices of the system, so bold had her actions been in the face of the city government, so embarrassing to the mayor and police department that her murder triggered screams of assassination! So the formerly silent city's citizens took to the streets and so did the intimidating presence of police.

Lasan and Anya had been visiting America for a month; staying with friends, sharing vegan meals, sewing together large black and red flags, drawing up posters and doing radio interviews. Their American hosts endeared themselves to the visitors from Ireland. Both Anya and Lasan had parents who were members of the Irish Republican Army, so activism ran through their blood like oxygen. The children of Irish revolutionaries took their fight against injustice to an international level upon hearing about the work that was being done in Chicago against globalization and state sponsored domestic terrorism.

Lasan and Anya knew the risk they were taking to travel to a political time bomb that is Chicago. They were just two foreign, idealistic white kids fighting back against racism, injustice and a corrupt system, while loving each other. They were known as the cute couple from Europe with thick Irish accents who were always either offering to help break down the system or kissing. Everybody in the organization loved them. Just days ago everything had been beautiful, almost as beautiful as the bright red splash of blood Lasan just wiped from his face.

Pushing again against the wall of humanity through the opening, Lasan extricated himself and hit the ground. He scooted away from the wall of chaos, scanning to see if a cop had witnessed his escape. Out the corner of his eye, he caught a glimpse of some of his comrades; Chrissy, Alexandra and the other Alexandra, the latter he recognized immediately as the Black girl he and Anya befriended before the protest. She was a close friend of the woman who'd been murdered. Lasan saw that all three were safely retreating from the violence, he wanted to yell to them concerning the whereabouts of Anya but they didn't see him.

"YOU!!! BACK OVER THE LINE!!!" A sprinting cop in full riot gear yelled at Lasan. Before he could even position his body to run, the cop grabbed him by the neck and a club came smashing hard into his chest. The wind flew from Lasan's lungs and he felt himself being dragged by his neck.

"THE FUCK...PIECE OF SHIT!!!!" The cops' voice rattled Lasan with its hatred and rage.

Suddenly, the cop let go of Lasan's neck, the club falling from his hand as he hit the ground. Lasan fell backwards next to the club. He saw an arm pick up the club but he couldn't make out anything else of the person who then raised the baton and started beating the officer.

"PUT IT DOWN MOTHER FUCKER!!!" the cop yelled.

CRACK!!! CRACK!!! CRACK!!! The unmistakable sound of a dense wooden club breaking the plastic face guard of a riot helmet.

Lasan's eyes finally focused to make out Alexandra number two pummeling the cop who was desperately reaching for something on his belt. He set a mental note to thank her later if they made it out of this alive. This young African American woman needed no help, but obviously the cop did.

Lasan picked himself up on wobbly legs and ran away, "GET AWAY ALEX!!" he screamed, looking back at her.

"JUST GO!!!" she yelled back.

A stench filled Lasan's nose; a cop had just thrown a gas canister nearby. One more thing to deal with. Coughing, limping slightly and clutching his chest, his black t-shirt stretched and torn, he saw his book bag in the street, stumbled to it and grabbed it. He then went back to surveying the scene for Anya. Had she gotten away? Is she waiting for me to make it to her? Is she safe?

FX NOZAKHERE

In his heart, Lasan felt optimism draining from his body like the blood spilling in the streets. He stumbled forward, trying to gain his balance and move faster so he wouldn't be the target of another riot cop.

The police pushed a crowd of protesters backward against a building. A few broke away and started running frantically through the street from the oncoming march of newly arrived riot police. They marched in a ten by eight formation down the street, their light blue helmets shining, shields glistening, uniforms jet black without dust, spit or blood. They were ready for battle and the weapons they were brandishing didn't look like the non-lethal weaponry of the riot cops the protesters were already painfully familiar with. Smoke from tear gas containers was everywhere, trash containers were turned over, spilling trash onto the street, an NBC media van was aflame.

Lasan's attention was forced to his left as another screaming crowd of protesters broke free from the wall and were scrambling away from pursuing riot cops. There was a stampede of human animals being attacked with police cattle prods. In the center was a crash of bodies tripping over one another, frantically trying to escape while riot cops stepped on people to get to other people. In the midst of the fray, Lasan recognized one of the trampled.

"ANYA!!!" He screamed.

Forgetting his own safety and multiple injuries, Lasan sprinted over to Anya, his body moving slower than he would have liked. The crowd had scattered, leaving behind only those who had fallen under their feet. Behind Lasan, a block away, was the impending wall of new and more lethal riot police. He ran to where Anya had fallen.

She'd hit the ground hard and turned her ankle almost ninety degrees. Her brown hair, which had come free of the bun she usually wore, was a mass of unruly curls and full of grime and ash. Her sky blue shirt was spotted with dirt and blood. The beautiful legs that Lasan loved to caress were now dirty and scuffed as Anya clutched her ankle. She quickly turned her head at the man approaching from her right.

"LASAN!!!" That one word conveyed all the fear, panic, pain, hope and relief coursing through her body.

" Oi'm 'ere! Can ye walk?! Are ye ok?!" Lasan rattled off the questions as he plopped on the ground beside her.

"Lasan..." Anya winced, holding back tears of pain, "... Oi'm not 'aving a guud time roi now. We proobably shud 'ave jist gone ter fecking Nee'agra Dells."

Lasan was stunned by Anya's unpredictable humor during chaos and chuckled. He was relieved to finally find her and letting out a sigh, he grabbed Anya for a hug.

"Dahm, oi wus scared! Oi didn't know wha ye were! An it's thee Wi'consin Dells." The wall of riot police were closing in, three hundred feet away.

"Oi'm roight wha Oi always am. Get'n fecking trampled..." Anya replied, wincing at the pain in her leg. She stopped and stared right into Lasan's eyes, almost as if she was ignoring the impending danger marching towards both. "..But dis is what we asked fer, dis is what oi wanted, makin' a difference with you." Anya's voice softened. The wall inched closer, one hundred ninety feet away.

"Ey, but Dis not a time to be romantic..." Lasan replied, wiping a wisp of errant hair from Anya's face. "..Am goin' ta move ye out da street..." Before Lasan could get another word out, Anya grabbed the back of his head, pulling him close.

"Wait, dis perfekt." The automatic action was a kiss. She held onto her man, in defiant of the war all around them, defiant of the bloodshed, defiant of the wall of police that was now ninety feet away. They didn't care. They laid on the ground in a bubble of protection, thinking only of this moment, another memory in what they were building, a long-storied life together, something to tell their grandchildren. The battles fought, the battles lost, the battles won; the love that was always present.

The riot police were sixteen feet away, clubs out, voices blaring under fierce helmets. Still engaged in their kiss, Anya and Lasan's eyes finally opened...the sky was gone! There was a flash of white light and an explosion. The ground under Lasan and Anya shook. There were screams...then silence. The terrible sound of something huge and mechanical smashed into the ground, its' electric roar drowning out all other sound.

Suddenly riot police helmets, clubs, boots and pieces of humans began raining from the sky. The street was dotted with the unmistakable sight of blood and human flesh. Pieces of concrete rolled about on the ground and gray smoke swirled in the wind, obscuring something metallic, animal-like and incredibly big. There it stood amid the raining blood, flesh and debris, glaring at the lovers.

"Lasan, wha...what in de 'ell is dat?!"

BE QUIET AND DRIVE

Work sucked tonight! The pressure, the hectic rush of my co-workers, the screw ups and the noise! It was unending. *God I'm so glad to be out of there*! So many times I'd wanted to tell people to shut the hell up! I swear I almost snapped.

After ten hours, plus overtime, of non-stop chatter from co-workers, I needed some extended time alone to relax. I didn't even care that it was one in the morning, I took the long route home; the very long route.

The stretch of road was new to me, somewhere south on Route 171. It was a thin two lane road leading through a thick canopy of trees like a forest. I'd never ventured this far just to go home but it was beautiful scenery and I needed something serene to focus on to get my mind out of the chatter mode. The township I was traveling through wasn't big at all, sitting on the southwest outskirts of Chicago.

It had once been a much more prosperous place, during the heyday of the big laboratory that had been the anchor of the town and brought in other businesses. When the lab left, the remaining businesses couldn't absorb the large drop in populace and had to vacate.

What remained was a town hurting bad but not totally defeated, the residents remaining doing what they could to keep the place alive. I had to give the people credit for trying to make it work despite the economic odds.

I would have felt even more compassion for them, had they not been a bunch of bigoted White folks blaming Blacks and Mexicans for their economic hardships. It's precisely that bigotry, subtle and covert, that kept my Black, female ass from staying too long in this area. So I drove the 35 mph speed limit, through dimly lit, empty streets, not trying to get pulled over for speeding.

The night air was cool and caressing, the sky, a beautiful dark blue and dotted with stars. The moon illuminated the areas not lit with artificial light with a faint blue. Every few seconds, on the side of the road, I saw a light post, a fire hydrant, a mailbox, then repeat. Not much else.

DuSable City

Some time passed, my mind drifted and my eyes closed for what seemed only a second. Upon opening them, there on the right side of the road, was a woman alone, in a flowing white dress and walking. I passed her, with nothing more than a slight wonder as to where she might be going, by herself, in the middle of the night. The question plagued me for a moment; it was simply too dangerous a world for a woman to be out alone in the dark like this. Hell, it's too dangerous for men!

I reasoned that maybe she had a short walk to where she was going or maybe someone was meeting her. I certainly hoped so. I knew all too well the pitfalls of being a woman alone in this predatory world. I brushed a baby loc from my face and continued deeper into the darkness that is the road ahead of me. I could see the residential area becoming more sparse the further I drove. Ahead of me is the blanket of forest. It's a slow approach but not before I passed one more light post, fire hydrant, mailbox, then nothing.

The darkness of the night swallowed the road, embracing my car in a thick cover so dense, I could barely see what lay before me. The headlights only penetrated a small bit of the night, making me uncomfortable, the bright yellow lane lines my only source of reassurance.

"Just follow the lines and you'll be alright." I spoke this aloud as much to fight off the heaviness I felt descending on me as to have the company of my on voice in the silent darkness.

My eyes became heavy again. As I peeked through the thin slits of my eyelids, there again was a woman walking, almost floating, on the side of the road. The same white dress flowing freely in the air. I slowed down to get a better look at her. She never made eye contact, but something about her made my senses come alive. Was she the same woman as before? Same dress, same hair, same walk and headed in the same direction. Puzzled, I drove on.

Minutes passed. Every few seconds on the side of the road, a speed sign, a guard rail, a homemade cross with flowers then repeat.

The hum of the engine relaxed me but this time I kept an

eye on the side of the road for what? Maybe another woman? Maybe I could get a better look? I shook my head and slowed down just a little, my eyes scanned the right side, darting back and forth between the road and the side of the road. There, the headlights caught a dim wisp of pale in the distance. I squinted, thinking *am I coming up on her again?*

I slowed the car almost to a crawl, barely 7 miles per hour. The closer I got, the dimmer it became, until the flutter of pale disappeared. Was it her? What was that?

Something bumped my side of the car near the window. I immediately jumped, jerking the steering wheel in the process! In the side view mirror, I glimpsed a full grown deer veering its' gallop away from the car to the left side of the road.

I turned my attention back to the road in front of me, moving the car back to the right side of the line. Yet, in the distance, I see more deer. They were on the opposite side of the road, slowly trotting in the same direction I was driving. I'd hoped the deer that bumped my car wasn't injured but I couldn't tell.

FX NOZAKHERE

The deer walking in front of my car appeared to not be bothered at all by the lights and engine. *Maybe I can speed up a bit to get alongside them to have a closer look at these beautiful creatures was my thought,* so, I did just that, ignoring the jarring scare I'd just received. I accelerated a bit to catch up, not considering how strange their apparent fearlessness really was.

Soon I was alongside these majestic beauties and it was just as I'd imagined, imposing. Yet, I noticed *these* deer did not turn to look at me, or speed away from my car. Strange that they weren't at all afraid...too late! I should have thought of that before.

The deer closest to my car suddenly turned to look at me... its face. SHIT, the other side of its face was completely gone! There was nothing but the remains of its skull with some bloody chunks of flesh still clinging to it. My eyes met its one glowing red left eye. Its mouth opened, letting out a horrible, guttural shriek while baring rotted teeth! My ears felt as if they were pierced by the animal's scream!

Another smaller deer came into view from the left side of

the rotted one, on its side was a giant gaping hole, its bloody rib cage exposed, broken and incomplete. Its entrails fell out from the wound with every step the deer took.

There was another shriek, this time it deafened my ears and I knew I had to get away. I leaned on the accelerator, leaving the scene as fast as possible. I could hear galloping speeding up behind me, but my car was faster. Soon, the gallops became faint until I heard them no longer.

"What the hell! How are they still alive?!" My ears are slowly recovering from the animals' cry, as if I'd just left a concert; everything sounded muffled.

"That woman! She's going to come across those deer.. they could be rabid!" The voice inside my head rang with concern but it was too late for me to do anything. I couldn't and wouldn't turn around now. I hoped to God she would be okay.

I waited for my hearing to normalize, during which I calmed down enough to continue driving. On the side of the road, I nervously passed...A speed limit sign, a guard rail, a homemade cross adorned with flowers and a picture of a small boy, then nothing.

How big was this forest? Finally, on the right side of the road, there's an opening through the trees. Then another, then another larger one.

While carefully driving, I tried to make out what was beyond the openings. It was a lake, the moon's light had revealed just enough of the shimmering water that I could make it out.

Seconds later, the trees and bushes reveal in their absence what they were hiding. It was indeed a lake, a big one. The still waters calmed my spirit. The things I'd seen so far had baffled me, so to witness this beauty was welcomed indeed.

I kept my eyes on the road but every few seconds, I'd turn to catch a glimpse of the lake. But this time, as I slowed to a crawl, I occasionally looked to make sure there were no strange animals running up on my left side.

Eyes forward on the road, glanced to my left, back to the road, then over to the water for a look.

Beautiful.

Eyes forward on the road, glanced to my left, back to the road, then over to the water for a look.

Calming.

Eyes forward on the road, glanced to my left, back to the road, then over to the water for a look.

Something rose out of the water. My eyes froze on this...what the hell was that?! A sizable shadowed figure rose out the water, hunched over, drooping, with a head and shoulders...arms, hands. I sped up. Fuck if I was sticking around to see the rest of whatever that was. The revving of the engine even sounded nervous.

"This is the most fucked up road I've ever been on! How do I get out of this damn forest?!" It came out in an angry rush before I'd even realized I was speaking out loud. I couldn't panic, there had to be an end and I needed to find it...quick!

I wanted to stop and look at the map in my trunk but after strange women walking, mutilated deer and crazy shit popping out of the damn water, all in a bigoted white neighborhood, I dared not stop. I had gas, I was wide awake and it was only a matter of time before I came to the end of this forest and back into civilization.

I sped up, dismissing the speed limit. A minute passed. On the side of the road I saw an "S curve ahead" sign, a damaged guard rail, roadkill. The road took a sharp turn, just as the sign indicated. I followed the headlights as they guided my way around another curve. Every little detail of the forest caught my eye and my imagination.

Was that another bloody deer?! No, just a tall bush. Was that another woman walking?! No, just light reflecting off paper caught in the wind. What the hell is that?! Oh, it's just a big, burned tree stump.

I leaned from one sharp curve into another, my eyes waiting to catch something that shouldn't be. I didn't want to psyche myself out, start seeing things that weren't really there but had I before? The woman? The thing emerging from the lake? The mutilated deer? Well, the deer had been real, that much I knew. Maybe all of it was real and I was just slee…

The cars' back tires slipped, I wasn't paying attention to my turns! The back end of the car dipped off the road into the forest floor, the car twisting around in the opposite direction. I pressed down on the brakes hard which caused the car to grind to a halt.

I sat for a second, heart drumming in my chest, but I continued my thought…maybe all of this was real and I'd just been sleepy? The car was halfway off the road. Was what I'd seen real? I'd just crashed. Shit, I was lost in thought and hadn't been paying attention. I was entirely too close to the edge of the road.

I leaned over to look out the passenger side window. Am I losing my mind? The car was fucking stuck and I was alone! Dammit, I had to pee. Bad.

I slowly let my foot off the brake and gently press on the accelerator, the car rocked forward but the back tires were spinning on mud or loose gravel or something. Whatever it was, it didn't offer enough traction to propel the car back onto the road.

"SHIT!" I banged my fist on the steering wheel. I didn't want to get out. I didn't want to get out. I didn't want to get out! But what was I going to do? I started looking through the car, the backseat, the floor, the glove compartment, searching for a weapon or a flashlight.

After throwing open the glove compartment, I didn't find a weapon but there was a flashlight. I grabbed it, tested the button and activated the light...thank God it worked. I turned it off immediately as not to attract any attention. A crashed car was enough noise, a blaring light in the dark forest was an invitation to whatever. By now I was convinced there was something about this forest, this situation, this experience that was the epitome of extra ordinary. Whatever was going on, I was scared to death!

I had to see how far off the road the car was. The view outside the driver's window was nothing but a canvas of pitch black, occasionally invaded by faint moonlight just bright enough to illuminate some detail of the thick woods and the lines on the road. The only sound was the wind gently moving tree branches and shaking leaves. I could smell the dampness of the lake, which bothered me because that meant I was close to it and thus close to whatever had come up out the water. The mere thought of that caused my heart to pound even harder in my chest.

Ok, I needed to get out the car to check the damage. I rolled up the window, unlocked the door, opened it...wait, I needed to turn on the flashlight first. Ok, ready, set...fuck, this light wasn't working. I hit the switch again and it blazed to life.

I flung open the door and immediately used the light to scan my surroundings. The flashlight showed me the forest, allowing my eyes to clearly see wherever I pointed the light. I gently closed the car door, trying to make as little noise as possible. I certainly didn't want anything sneaking into the damn car through a neglected open door.

To my left was the edge of the road, where the back of the car disappeared into the shadows. I ordered my steps carefully, pointing the light at the back of the car then down to the wheels, then to the ground then...nothing. The car was damn near teetering over a steep ledge and at the bottom, more darkness. It had to be just trees and...

FX NOZAKHERE
"RRRROOOOOOAAAAARRRRGGGHHH!!!"

"What the fuck was that?!" I turned quickly and shot the flashlight in every direction my head turned, my entire body tensing. The guttural roar still echoed in the night but now, along with it, was the rustling of leaves and the unmistakable sound of rapid footsteps through foliage. I didn't know what to expect so I shined the flashlight in the direction of the rustling. Could I get to a weapon in the car? Fuck, what weapon?!

From the dense woods, what appeared to be a human figure emerged. I aimed the flashlight at the figure, but as soon as the light hit, the space around it turned into a bright, almost blue haze. It spoke, some undecipherable language, very fast and forcefully.

"Stay the hell away!!" I yelled. The figure paused its advancement, still speaking its strange language. It wasn't Spanish, or German, or Patois, but something I'd never even heard..

"Mahkatew ihkwewa....nakwewa!" The voice was deep

and masculine. The darkness faded from the figure and I put my flashlight down; the haze from around it disappeared.

By then, I was frozen with fear and confusion. Confused as to why I was still standing in the same spot after hearing what I'd just heard and seeing what I was seeing.

"Nakwewa!" The voice became more impatient as it stepped from the darkness and I started to make out details of this figure. A red something over the shoulder, what looked like a beige shirt with a collar and a head...a bald head with a face decorated with colored lines of paint. The figure was clearly in the moonlight now. My fear began to recede as I stared in disbelief at what looked like a man with copper skin and deep lines in a face that seemed to be showing what I felt was concern.

Hanging from his ears were piercings and rings that I'd never seen before. I could see now that the red was a sash-like piece of fabric thrown over his shoulder, contrasting with his beige shirt and brown pants. All his clothing was like nothing I'd ever seen before, yet there was something oddly familiar about this person standing before me.

His eyes scanned me up and down, he raised his hand as if to carefully but urgently motion me away. I squinted my eyes and lowered the flashlight; it didn't seem to be needed around him anyway. Weird though.

"Who are you?!" I nervously uttered, but before the copper colored man could answer, another roar emitted from the distance. Not as loud as the first but this time accompanied by the sound of trees bending and cracking. I tilted my head up at the same time as the man and we both witnessed the black outline of a tree, against the dark sky, shake and fall. He turned to me, uttered something then frantically pointed behind me, just as a hand grabbed my arm from behind.

"SHIT?!" I snatched my arm away and whirled to see several dark figures in the road, all copper colored men wearing clothes similar to the one now standing behind me.

"There are more of you?!" I yelled but they were on the move.

They motioned for me to run in the direction they were

already moving in. The first man I'd encountered ran past me and uttered something else; I wasn't staying around to try to figure out the language, I just started running. Whatever was making those noises and knocking down tall ass trees was much more of a concern to me than these seemingly benign people I was now following.

So here I was, running down the road in a forest, at night, behind strange people who'd appeared out of nowhere. While I should have been thinking of these men having me in a vulnerable position, it was clear we were all trying to escape some big roaring thing. *Fuck that car, I'll come back to it. Fuck my life's problems, I'll get back to them once I **save** my life!*

The men were all faster than me, speaking their language under their breaths, their feet smacking the concrete while the sound of trees rustling in the distance could be heard behind us. I could faintly hear the sound of footsteps from whatever that thing was hitting the ground. My eyes were beginning to adjust to the night enough to see the road more clearly, so I switched off the flashlight. No need bringing visual attention to me, to us.

A minute passed...

On the side of the road, we run past...a felled tree, a bent speed limit sign, more roadkill.

Suddenly, they veer off to the left, into an opening in the woods. The original man I'd met stopped at the entrance and beckoned me to hurry with hand gestures. I had to slow down, the darkness of what I was about to enter was unsettling.

"I can't see...what you want me to....dammit!"

"WWRRRRRAAAAAAOOOOOORRRR!!!!"

"Shit! It's closer!!!" I placed my hands over my brow and rushed into the woods on the side of the road. The copper colored man guided me through by placing his hand gently on my back, occasionally grabbing my shirt to steer me in the right direction. I was stumbling over rocks, moving as fast as I could through sharp, branch filled blackness. The sound of branches cracking, leaves being brushed, and several people pounding the ground hard was all an indication of the undeniable seriousness of this situation!

Among all the frantic sounds, I could faintly hear the

other runners speaking their strange language under their breaths; they were afraid, I could tell. One of the copper colored men said something louder in their language. Our collective pace slowed, as they continued to speak to each other. The original copper colored man behind me adds to whatever conversation they were having. I could only wonder as to what they could be saying to each other. An assessment of the danger? Where they were going? Should we ask this Black woman for a ride out of here?

"Whoa, was that a blue light flickering?" It flashed quickly, almost like a police light. I could only hope the racist police were there to help. Shit, it was so weird, they probably wouldn't have the time nor opportunity to harass this Black woman. But this light was flickering more and more in the direction we were heading. The closer we got, the more of it I could see. It was just one more strange thing in what was supposed to be a quiet drive home from work. Why am I steadily walking towards this strange light, with these strange men, speaking their strange language, all while being chased by something really big, loud, and strange?

By now, the light had ceased its flickering and become a constant glow, only dissected by the trees and branches that obscured my view of it. The group that ran with me didn't seem to be too bothered by the presence of this glow. In fact, they were walking towards it, seemingly unafraid of this beautiful but mysterious light. However, I'd had enough of the strange shit tonight. My walk slowed and my body language was unenthusiastic about the prospect of further advancement into more unexplained happenings. If that was the case, then why couldn't I stop walking towards it? It was as though we were all being drawn to this mysterious illumination.

All of the copper colored men were now in front of me, slowly advancing towards the light. The original copper man turned back to me, again speaking in his language. The puzzlement on my face must have been easy to read because his facial expression became one of concern. He reached out his hand and beckoned me further. My feet, although hesitant, had not completely stopped.

My curiosity started to take over, "What the hell is that?!"

I ask him. Still, he reached out for me to move closer.

There is an opening in the woods, pretty big, with tall beige weeds, thick green plants and a few bushes. All of it lit by the light I now clearly see is emanating from a big round, pulsating bright blue circle just suspended there, a little bit off the ground. It makes no sound, at least none that I can hear.

I'm frozen at what I'm seeing. Momentarily, I think back to the danger we were running from but this has me completely captivated. My mouth dropped and I know my eyes were huge. My heart...I felt like I was about to have a heart attack, it was beating so fast. Yet, despite what I could see as immediate danger in this situation, there was...a beauty to it. I felt an eeriness but also I felt an inner warmth, caring and compassion.

The copper colored men talked among themselves and occasionally looked back at me. The original man walked back to me, the look on his face made me feel more at peace. If he was speaking to me, I couldn't tell, I was paying too much attention to a growing sensation within me. My head filled with memories. I picked up a familiar smell, a scent I used to love...what was happening?

My eyes teared up a bit and I didn't know why. The copper colored man continued to speak to me but I...hold up a minute. From the bright blue circle, a figure stepped onto the forest floor. The copper colored man followed my eyes, turning his head.

The figure, emerging from the circle of light...I couldn't see clearly. Wait! It walked away from the light, its' form gradually becoming more and more familiar, until I could see it better.

My mind and heart are racing...

Is that...MY...MY MOTHER?! MY DEAD MOTHER?!

DADDY ISSUES

"Daddy, I don't want you to go!" Maryam cried, as her little four and a half year old feet carried her across the dimly lit living room, as fast as possible, and propelled her into her father's arms. Her tears stained his white shirt as she buried her small face in his shoulder. The father embraced his daughter tightly, tears welling up in his eyes. He thought about how his decisions brought about these consequences. What he'd never considered possible was now crushing the hope out of his daughters' little body. She wailed at the same time he let out a weak sigh.

Her father had been in and out of trouble most his young life; the first three years of her life were scattered with his presence. If it wasn't jail, it was him hiding from trouble that he felt would harm his family. Never did he take into account the biggest harm was his absence. Missed birthdays, first words, first steps; a little girl disappointed over and over again. However, the past year things had been different.

Standing in the unlit portion of the dining room was

Maryam's mother. She'd never wanted to be a single mom; most women don't. Yet, she had recovered from heartbreaks, forgave transgressions and supported Malik when she felt he didn't really deserve it. All she wanted, mainly, was a father for her precious little girl. A little girl she was now witnessing go through yet another disappointing heartbreak, which in turn, was breaking hers… again.

"Hey sweet girl, look at me baby." The father spoke softly into her ear. He tried to gently pull her away so he could see her face but she wouldn't budge. Instead she let out a numbing howl.

"Nooooooo!" Again he gently tugged, only to be met with the resisting strength of an upset four year old. Eventually, she relented and looked up at him, her tears accentuating her dark brown cheeks and running to pool around the neckline of her Storm X-Men shirt.

"You're going to ruin your favorite shirt.." the father placed her on the floor, got down on his knees and look his daughter in the eyes, knowing this would be the last time.

"..I want to come back and see you...I hope to come back to see you, but every day I had with you was the best day of my life. You bring me so much jo...joy." His voice cracked on the last word.

"While I'm gone, I need you to remember some things ok..." Maryam barely nodded her head, her little afro puff bobbing as she did so. He lip poked out along with her little tummy.

"..You're becoming a big girl and you gotta start doin' big girl things now, being responsible. You have to promise me you'll help your mama. Can you promise me that?" Maryam nods her little head while wiping tears.

"Ok good, because your mama loves you and there's gonna be times when she'll need your help, so you can't be actin' up when y'all are out or when you start school." Maryam again nodded yes.

The father paused, searching for what to say to a little girl he'd only become familiar with in the past eleven months. He briefly looked over to the mother, who looked at him with disappointment and worry before turning back to the window where she stood waiting.

"Do you remember the things we talked about? The three things I taught you?" He asked quietly.

"Yes." Maryam replied sheepishly.

"Tell me. I need to know *you* know these things before…" he paused, forcing back the tears, "…before I go."

Maryam's eyes pointed up and to the left, her tiny hands fidgeted then flopped down to her sides. Her round, brown cheeks streaked with tears.

" I…I have to protect myself, because…because of boys…dey will try to hurt me." He father smiled sadly.

"Ok…what else did you learn?" She thought for a minute.

"My dark bwown skin is bootiful…Blaaack is bootiful. Uhh…don't be 'shamed cuz of being dark skinneded. Dat I come from…a long hewitage of bootiful, great people who all look like, like me and you and mommy." She finished with an air of pride in herself.

"And what else Maryam baby?" Maryam fidgeted again, wiped a tear from her eye, and continued reciting her last life lesson.

"I.....I aaaammm...."

"Come on... you remember it." Malik encouraged her.

"I am..." her eyes looked up and to the side as if searching for the word to remember.

"In...invinsibal. I am invisinbal..." she spoke with more confidence as her mind latched on to the word.

"..In life, nothing can defeat me...umm...if I believe in mahself." Malik released a chuckle.

"Invincible. You are invincible."

Maryam's round face was one of revelation as she repeated the word. "Invincibal. I'm invincibal."

"Good baby, good. No matter how hard your life gets, no matter what bad things may happen, never let it beat you. Know that it won't last and that you will be alright. Never give up on yourself."

Maryam's little voice responded, "Okay daddy..."then a confused look emerged on Maryam's face before she finally said "...But daddy, who will p'tect me from the monsters in the worl'? You going away!"

The father took his daughter's her tiny hands, "Listen to me baby, there is no monster that is more powerful than you... there is nothing in this world that's more powerful than you. You are strong, you are smart, you are brave. That's what being invincible means. Do you understand?"

Maryam's eyes reflected on what her father said, "Yes."

At that moment, red and blue lights cut through the window into the apartment. With that, a subtle rumble shook the tables and cabinets of the apartment, invading the last moment between a father and his daughter. The mother, while wiping tears, gasped at the presence outside and slowly backed away from the window, never taking her eyes off what was going on outside.

DuSableCity

"They're here!" The mother exclaimed as she nervously reached out her hand for Maryam. The father, knowing what was coming next, immediately pulled his daughter in for one last hug.

"I'm so sorry, I love you so much Maryam."

"It'll be ok. I love you too daddy." She was already learning.

The father stood, still holding Maryam's hand as the mother came to take her other hand, leading her away. They were waiting outside for him.

A heavy weight descended on him as he took his first step towards the door. Every step became harder, each one bringing up a memory. He looked over to the woman with whom he conceived a daughter. He remembered the good times, the trying times and thought how unfortunate it was that the bad times outnumbered the good. He still loved her and he knew she loved him. She was a good mother and despite all the bad times, she'd still given him many chances to be the father Maryam needed.

It was this thought that flooded his mind and caused the

tears to finally flow. He'd been given the opportunity numerous times and in those times, he'd done his best. He'd come through except the one time it really mattered, the one time she'd really needed him; the one time he'd really needed her. The bad luck of his DNA had changed their lives forever. He was being taken away, again, leaving this brilliant little girl without a father just like so many others.

His train of thought stopped as he grabbed the doorknob, he paused. His daughter still had the look of sadness on her face, the mother had the look of fear.

"Malik…" she whispered, motioning as if she wanted to reach out to him and snatch him back from what was on the other side of the door.

He barely heard her call his name, already opening the door and suddenly entranced by the blue, red and white lights flickering on his brown face and illuminating the apartment. He put his hand over his brow and proceeded out the door. It was a show of force outside.

DuSable City

The craft hovered a few inches above ground. There was no engine noise, only a subtle, rhythmic hum. The length and width encompassed the entire park across the street from the apartment complex. It was basically a flying building overshadowing the apartment and totally blocked the view of everything across Levine Park. Malik had often wondered if he'd ever see a flying saucer, or at least that's what they were called. But, there was nothing "saucer" about this.

Sleek in its design, a sharp front with a loaded rear, complete with what looked like a spoiler structure and wings. The entire outside was adorned with rhythmic, pulsating lights shaped in straight lines and orbs. It reminded Malik of a Christmas tree, lying sideways, from hell. For him it was foreboding and terrifyingly beautiful.

Malik stopped his progress in the front courtyard and turned back to see if Maryam and her mother were a safe enough distance away from the door and windows. To his dread, they both were frozen with their mouths open at the window.

He waved his arms, "Get away! Get away from the

window!" But Maryam and her mother were too awestruck to even notice Malik.

"Get away from the window!!!" He screamed just as the side of the craft opened.

Malik cupped his hand around his mouth, hoping in vain that his voice would carry over the crafts hum and to Maryam and her mother's ears.

"Get away from the window!!!"A figure appeared and walked up slowly behind Malik.

Still yelling, Malik trying not endanger his family by antagonizing the beings from the craft, he started to panic and even contemplated running back onto the apartment. In one last desperate attempt to spare them, he screamed again.

"Please get away from…"

"They are fine. We will not harm them." A calm, deeply etheric voice emanated from behind Malik. Startled, he jolted around quickly and immediately turned his head upward. It was but a silhouette, back lit by the magnificence of the craft. It had a humanoid outline but Malik could not tell if it was a man or a

woman, but the voice was unmistakably feminine.

"Maaaleek...we are here for you." A large arm stretched

from the silhouette down towards Malik, it's surface seemed

metallic and yet it moved like skin, the hand at the end of the arm

was tipped with five sharply pointed tips. It's color seemed to

change from blue to black with every slight move. Malik moved

to guard his head and his hunched shoulders as soon as he saw the

arm come towards him.

"Resist not, fear not." The feminine voice reassured Malik

with a combination of softness and power. The hand gently

landed on Malik's left shoulder, he shook at its touch. The being

guided him towards the lighted craft, it stepped to the side and

raised its other large arm as if to say welcome, this way. This time,

as it moved to the side to make way for Malik, the light from the

craft gave him a chance to see more of what was before him.

His eyes peered upward, surveying this creature. He could

barely see it because of the luminescence of the light. One thing

was sure, it was humanoid and tall, he knew that from the news reports. However, this one was affixed with what appeared to be a very dark plated armor and a female shape could be made out.

Malik held his hand to his brow to block some of the light from his vision. He thought to himself *it has on a mask, not a helmet. Its face is a blank glass…what the hell is that? What does it look like without this armor? Where are they really from?"* How *am I connected to these things?!*

"Your questions will be answered Maaleek." The utterance from the creature and its seeming invasion of his mind shook Malik to his soul. He hesitated as he turned toward the craft. He took a deep breath and continued a slow walk to it.

As he approached the craft's opening, the creature walking behind him turned its head back to the house and affixed its gaze upon Maryam and her mother.

"I see you have a girl child," turning its head slowly back to Malik, "…maybe we come back for her."

Upon hearing this, Malik immediately stopped at opening of the craft, his body flooded with instant terror. He turned to the creature, "NO! It was me and only me! That is what I agreed to!"

For the first time Malik's powerlessness left him and defiance replaced it.

"Your genes are our genes and she is part of you, twenty three parts. We will take her as well…in time." The confidence of the creature was only surpassed by its' authoritative compulsion, a tone verbalized through an electronic feminine voice that filled Malik with dread.

He looked back at the apartment building. Finding Maryam's little silhouette in the first floor window, he readied his body to push past the creature and run, run out on the deal because for him it was now off the table. He had to get back to his daughter, he was now ready to fight and die for her, damn it all.

Malik took two quick steps and the being uttered, "Take him." A flash of light hissed through the air and engulfed him, a frozen face of panic was the last bit of his body to disappeared within the light, then it faded. The being stood alone, still looking at where Malik had just stood. It turned its head toward the window where Maryam and her mother were now dissolving into fits of tears. It took a step in the direction of the apartment, stopped and simply stared at the two human forms for a few seconds. The mother's heart almost literally skipped several beats.

The being tilted its head up slightly as if hearing something in the night. Taking a step, it turned, walking back to the opening in the craft.

Once entered, the light that emanated from inside disappeared as a door rose to a closed position. A loud, bass hum vibrated through the entire Austin neighborhood as the craft gently rose from the park grounds until it was a sizable distance from the surface. It turned eastward, leveled up with more lights glowing from its rear and swiftly flew upward, until its immense size became a mere dot in a brightening, pre-dawn sky. Then there were no more lights. It was gone...

Carrying with it all Maryam's hopes.

CHURCH HATS

He skipped down the steps one by one, carefully hitting every step until he landed at the bottom. While quickly making his way to the door leading to the outside of his complex, he noticed some voices. Through the door window, he saw a peach colored hat with lace. Careful not to fling the door open too aggressively, he pulled the door easily and greeted the building's visitors.

"Oh hey there young fella!" A lady greeted him with a smile on her face. "Looks like we're right on time...see how that works y'all?!" She looked to two other ladies, both with brightly colored dresses. Upon their regally graying heads were the capstones representing decades of respectable church style clothing. An element of the Black experience that is emblematic of class, sophistication and moral uprightness; the church hat.

Each one of their hats matched the bright colors of their clothing, which were equally classy and sophisticated. One lady was regal in burgundy, one adorned in light green and one ornate in peach. All women were just entering their senior years, the oldest was Deb being 63, Cheryl 62 and Laney 61.

"I guess so...hello ladies!" The man smiled as he held the door for the elders. "You all have a great day!"

"Why thank you young man! So sweet!"

"Thank ya feller." Another chimed in.

"Thank you very much," replied the last.

The hallway was glowing from the afternoon sun shining its light through the thick amber colored windows. The heat from the reflective sunlight warmed the stairwell just enough to cause a little sweat but not anything unbearable. The foyer was clean. The rug, while a little worn, was vacuumed. A slight ammonia smell was evidence of someone spraying the windows with some type of glass cleaner. A few envelopes of mail and a magazine sat atop the mailbox and above that was a bulletin board. Pinned on the board were announcements for the residents of the building; birthdays, lawn services and a missing persons flyer.

All three seniors filed in, carrying purses and each, a

large canvas bag. Laney looked up and counted, "One, two, three...we're on the third floor you all. Everyone ok?"

"Well, the mind is willin' but the flesh gotta do its part." Deb chuckled as she led the way, stopping off to glance over the missing persons' poster. She shook her head and whispered "Lawd" to herself and proceeded towards the first set of stairs going. Right behind her, laughing, was Cheryl.

"Girl, let me tell you..." they all were strained, climbing the stairs slowly, "...my nephew started me doing exercises in the gym to get the dust out of my joints. I figured..." Cheryl took a breath before she took another step, "...I have to be in some kind of shape for the type of work I do."

"I know that's right." Laney slowly chimed in, the last one up the stairs.

"Your nephew..." Deb inquired, "...is he the one going to college in Florida?"

"You thinkin' bout Darnell, my other nephew, lil' chocolate boy...'member him?" Cheryl replied, while moving slowly up the stairs.

"Oh yeeeeeaaah, that little chocolate baby! Ahhhh hehehehehe!" Deb responded, as she gripped the railing on the side of the stairs. "That boy is a beautiful, dark-skinned chile."

Cheryl laughed, "Yes he is and doing the family proud."

"Not much of that anymore I'm afraid." Laney chimed in sadly, as she herself carefully selected each step.

"Not much of what Laney?" Deb asked.

"Pride. Being proud of something our children did. I just get so tired of hearin' bout some of this mess goin' on." Laney's voice huffed.

"Lord I know..." Cheryl replied. "...But I read a report somewhere, I don't remember where, saying there are more Black men in prison than in college?"

Laney's voice lifted, "you know, I heard about that too..." she caught her breath while pausing on the stairs, "...but there's a caveat to that, errr, situation..." Deb and Cheryl were half way up the next flight of stairs when they paused and turned to give their full attention to their friend as she continued.

"...What that statistic doesn't take into account is that it's just about college age Black boys. There are more Black boys in prison at that age...just in the college age, which is what?"

"Oh, uhm...eighteen, nineteen, to their early twenties." Cheryl added.

Laney pointed to Cheryl in agreement, "Right! That age group may have more men in college than prison but overall, yeah, there are a lot more of our Black men in prison."

"Well, I guess it makes sense, but why...why screw with the statistic?" Deb asked, as she started the climb back up the stairs.

"To make us feel hopeless," Laney answered, as she also started her way back up.

"Or inferior," Cheryl added, as she resumed taking her steps.

"Or maybe just to sensationalize the statistic...the...shit how long are these stairs?!" Deb chuckled, as she let out an exasperated sigh.

"I know it's only been a minute but it already feels like an hour!"

"Come on now y'all, it's not much longer... jus' a little bit mo."

All three managed laughter in between breaths from their climb. Their banter filled the empty space in the staircase as light from the sun beamed on every landing, making the air seem warmer with each ascension. Knee joints popped, shaking hands gripped handrails, and everything from a Jet magazine to a church fan was used to wave away the heat. But, no matter the discomfort, Laney's peach colored prize, with its big brim, stayed elegantly perched upon her head. Deb's burgundy bolero, with its lush, black band, stayed perfectly mounted. While, Cheryl's light green headpiece crowned her head like a halo. Despite their present condition, their elegance was evident.

"Ok, this is the last flight comin' up." Deb announced

"It wasn't that bad." Cheryl added.

"Everybody here doesn't have a trainer Cheryl." Laney responded.

"But you did good girl!" Deb responded joyfully..

"Yes you did Laney." Cheryl agreed.

"You used to get all out of breath, coughing and wheezing and what-not." Deb continued.

"Quitting smoking does wonders…" Laney responded.

"And I'm still proud of you for that!" Deb said excitedly.

"…Now I just smoke weed." Laney finished.

"Oh, okaaay." Deb replied surprised.

"Right Cheryl?" Laney looked at Cheryl, giving her a wink.

Smiling, Cheryl replied "Indeed Laney." It appeared the proverbial cat was out of the bag.

"Wait…" Deb interjected, "Y'all both are smoking that wacky weed?"

Laney and Cheryl looked at each other, then looked back

at Deb, "Well, yeah..." Cheryl responded.

"When did you two start doin' that?!" Deb's voice resonated with shock.

"Well, what..." Cheryl paused, "...only about a month ago."

"Y'all been smoking weed for a month?" Deb replied.

"Yeah, more or less...usually right after church." Laney added.

"After chur...y'all...wait..." Deb looked at her friends with a mixture of awe and anger. All three had gathered at the top of the last landing.

"You Cheech and Chong heifas been smokin' weed, after church and didn't tell me?!" She said, her head cocked to the side and her eye brows raised.

"We didn't know if you would want to do something like that. I mean, we were going to tell you...eventually, but we actually didn't think you'd like it, being so involved in the church and all," Cheryl replied.

"The same church we all go to Cheryl!" Deb's voice raised slightly, a smirk forming on her face.

"Ok right, ssssssooooo...what? Are you mad at us?" Laney asked.

Deb looked at her friend. "Chile, I started smoking weed two weeks ago!"

"What?!" Cheryl injected, holding back a laugh.

"We could have been smoking together if y'all had told me!" Deb added indignantly.

"We honestly didn't think *you'd* like doin that. Guess we were wrong," Cheryl said, still holding back a laugh.

"Where you get weed from Deb?" Laney inquired, one raised eyebrow.

"Probably the same person you got yours from." Deb answered, her hands on her hips.

Cheryl and Laney looked at each other, once Laney saw Cheryl trying to keep from laughing, a smirk crossed her face. "Janice?" Laney sheepishly asked.

" Yes Laney, the choir director!" Deb threw up her hands as she turned towards a door near the stairs. Cheryl and Laney finally burst out laughing.

"Well Laney, you should still come workout with me some time. It'll make ya feel even betta." Cheryl added.

"After this, I may...what say you Deb?" Laney's voice heightened.

"Huh? What's that?" Deb replied.

"Workout with me and Cheryl some time and have a little smoke together...Sister Deb?" asked Laney.

Deb was distracted. Her focus momentarily taken by the search for the apartment they were heading to. She closed her eyes, shook her head yes and waved her pointed finger in the air.

"Oh, that would be nice. Haven't done much....exercising in...a...while."

Deb's voice trailed off. Her eyes opened wider, struggling to read the numbers that were obscured by shadows made by the sunlight and old labels that had worn down over time.

"Here…this must be it right here…and it is. Ladies." Deb turned to her friends and lowered her voice as she gave out the final charges.

"Ok, let's get it together. He should be home…at least I hope he's home."

Cheryl responded "He is…I just heard something." Deb looked to Laney with a raised eyebrow,

"Laney?" Laney nodded in confident approval.

"Okay." Deb turned to the door, straightening her hat.

Laney and Cheryl both checked their respective hats at the same time, then Deb knocked on the door. No response, no sound from the other side. Deb knocked again, this time harder. From inside, there was the sound of muffled shuffling and a cup falling to the floor.

"Tony?!" Deb announced with authority. Again, there was silence. Seconds later, the unmistakable sound of sock covered footsteps shuffled towards the door,

"Deb?" a male voice quietly inquired.

"Yes, it's me Tony. I have friends with me...you know them." The loud sound of a top lock being disengaged invaded the quiet hallway. It was followed by the lesser rustling sound of the second lock.

The door opened and a stifling odor greeted the ladies, along with a man in blue jeans and a stained white t-shirt. His afro was unkempt and he hadn't shaved in days. The look on his fifty nine year old face was initially one of fear, but upon hearing all three ladies greet him, a visible relief flooded his countenance.

"Hey y'all...co...come on in." Tony replied in a low voice as he stepped to the side, allowing each woman to enter.

"Tony, what have you been doing in here?!" The concern in Deb's voice was evident. The apartment was a disheveled mess, matching the resident. Trash was spread about on the floor near an overflowing garbage can, open bottles of beer, most of them half empty, littered ever inch of table top. Newspapers, fast food bags and numerous medicine bottles were erratically placed everywhere. The strange odor hinted at Tony's downward spiral.

"Deb…uhhh…ladies, y'all want some water or a beer?"

Tony asked, never making eye contact with any one of the women.

Instead, looking down and turning as if looking for something.

His twitching and fidgeting caused Laney to stare at him with

hard eyes.

"Hell no!" She responded, while looking him up and

down. Cheryl gave her a rebuking look. Laney shrugged her

shoulders and waved Cheryl's stare off.

"Ha…have a seat…" Tony's speech was a bit slurred and

he was obviously nervous about something. He lowered himself

onto the love-seat, never bothering to remove the old newspapers

from the cushion, "…what can I do fo…for ya?"

Deb cleared off a small section of the stained recliner

across from Tony and bravely sat down, hovering off the edge.

"Tony, suga', I'm worried about you. How many times

have I told you that no matter what you're goin' through, you can

come to me…I can help."

Tony interrupted, "I know. I know! I just…Debbie, Cher,

Lane...I'm jus been havin' a hard time lately..." Cheryl walked over to Tony, putting her arm around his shoulders and he jumped slightly. His eyes met hers briefly then turned back to Deb.

"Then tell us what's wrong...we're here now." Cheryl said softly, while giving Tony a slight hug. Laney finally sat across from Tony and Cheryl, a look of deep concern on her face. Deb took off her church hat, briefly fanned herself with it and stood up.

"We're going to help you because you cannot go on living like this." she said firmly.

"Thank G....God for you Deb, for all a y'all. I...I don't know." Tony's voice stumbled over thoughts and words. He scratched his head until, ultimately, a slight smile came to his lips. Despite that, his eyes revealed a deep sadness. He looked away to the window, his eyes squinting a bit at the daylight shining through the blinds. He sat still for a few seconds.

"You know that big building that the Eisenhower Expressway goes through?" He asked no one in particular.

Cheryl answered, "The old post office building?"

DuSable City

"Yeah. I...I remember, when I was a little boy..." Tony wiped his nose and scratched his graying head.

"...No," he continued, "...I wuz, thirteen maybe fourteen when my daddy used to drive through and undaneath that building. I was always amazed by how big it was. I mean, it's so big a whole highway fits right through it, you know. I knew...I knew then I wanted to build buildings like that one. Most people don't know by then but I knew..." His eyes showed that his mind had drifted to another time.

"...I wanted to build buildings, skyscrapers, even cities. I wanted to...build Chicago. A little Black boy from South Shore was going to revolutionize architecture." He sniffed, put his hand over his mouth then coughed. Still staring out the window, occasionally looking at Deb, he continued.

"My momma wanted me to do that, my daddy, he wanted something else but he eventually became 'down with it' as the kids now-a-days say..."

He smiled, slightly. "It was around that time that the urges started. I tried to ignore them but it eventually became an addiction. For a long time I ignored 'em but after a while…I just couldn't."

"Tony…" Deb interjected softly.

"It ruined my damn life!" Tony sobbed, inhaled and fell silent as he lowered his head down. "I've been out of control for a long time, I need help. I know that now."

"Is it too far gone? Do you want help Tony? We can help you with that." Deb concluded.

"Cheryl, move to your left, just a lil bit." Laney politely requested.

"Oh, sure." Cheryl scooted her body accordingly.

BAM!!!!!

"Oh!" The man's head snapped back. Chunks of red exploded from the back of his head. His body slumped. It was quiet, the echo from the shot ended. Cheryl and Deb looked at Laney.

"Oh dammit! I forgot to put the silencer on." Laney

lamented.

"Laney, you got to be more careful!" Deb's voice rang with chastisement. She immediately walked over to the window, pulling the blinds apart just enough to see the activity on the street. Some people stopped and looked up towards all the buildings around them, others turned their heads quickly while jogging away from the area. The rest looked around and quickened their steps.

Scanning the area, Deb caught the eyes of three young women, one dressed in a skull cap, black shirt and jeans by the tree, another in jeans and a White Sox baseball t-shirt by the front door and the last dressed in a brown sundress sitting on a bench. All three returned glances up at the window Deb was looking out of, then they all looked away, unaffected.

"Well?" Cheryl nervously asked.

"We're good. People are just going bout' their business."

"And our girls?" Cheryl added.

"They're fine...at their posts." Deb answered coldly. She

released the blinds and walked over to the scene. A collective sigh went through the room.

With raised eyebrows, Laney discreetly released the cartridge from the nine millimeter, emptied the chamber and placed the collective pieces of the tool of destruction gently into her purse, careful not to leave her finger near the trigger.

"I thought you were gonna use the snub nose revolver?"

"Did any blood get on you Cheryl?"

"Somebody in the building had to hear that."

"No, there's no blood on me, but that wall..." There was silence. Each one looked around the apartment from where they stood. Cheryl looked over at what used to be Tony's head.

"That poor muthafucka," she whispered. There was silence again.

"Well, let's get started," said Deb. She suddenly walked through the unit, perusing through garbage cans, into the bathroom, through the cabinets, into the bedroom; through the drawers. Finally, she made her way back to the living room, the scene of everything. Laney and Cheryl had already started pulling items out of their respective bags, a sense of urgency in their motions.

Unfazed by their movements, Deb made a b-line through the living room, momentarily stumbling over some personal belongings of Tony's strewn about on the floor.

"Dammit Tony," she mumbled, as she regained her balance. She stopped at the last area of her search, the kitchen. The sound of cabinet doors opening and slamming came from the kitchen while Laney and Cheryl pulled out plastic spray bottles.

Deb kept at it, searching through the garbage, opening the oven door, looking behind the stove and mini microwave. A few beads of sweat started to form her brow, she felt them and wiped them away with a handkerchief from her pant pocket.

"How y'all doing out there?" She inquired, never breaking her pace. Laney, now wearing a surgical face mask and holding a towel, returned a muffled, "We're good!"

Deb continued her near frantic search, never breaking her

stride to listen to Laney's response. Her senior body moved in such a way it seemed to have forgotten the fatigue from three flights of stairs it had climbed. She opened a floor cabinet, peered in for a few seconds, then slowly stood up, closing it with a look of concentration.

Standing for a few seconds, she kept her hands on the knob while perusing the kitchen, her eyebrows were in a downward position indicating serious thought. *Where else?* Deb thought to herself as her eyes caught the most obvious object in the kitchen, the refrigerator. Deb slowly turned towards it, only taking two steps before standing in front of it; the kitchen was that small. She grabbed the handle refrigerator then paused, not immediately opening it. Instead, her eyes peered at the icebox door almost as if she were staring *through* it. Releasing the handle, she reached up slowly to grabbed the handle of the top freezer.

Again, she paused.

She could hear Cheryl and Laney moving working in the living room, they were already far along in their progress. She could smell the chemicals they were using to drown out the previously overwhelming smell in the apartment.

"Y'all might need to open a window out there, air it out."

"Good idea, we will."

Her grip on the freezer handle tightened; she pulled it open. Cold air wafted out, instantly leaving whiffs of condensation on her face. Her eyes cased the small section and rested on a particular item. Her expression changed from search mode to one of satisfied discovery. She uncovered what she'd come for.

Buried underneath popsicles, frozen veggie burgers and Baldwin's Neapolitan Ice Cream and wrapped in clear plastic, was a human hand. It was small with dried blood frozen on the surface of the skin, staining the plastic.

Without missing a beat, Deb slowly started moving items from on top of the hand. A human head suddenly appeared, it too was wrapped in plastic. A frozen afro, a mouth agape in a frozen scream and eyes frozen in terror stared out at her. Deb didn't move, her eyes transfixed on her discovery.

"Ladies.....I found him."

The sign downstairs read:

"MISSING CHILD

HELP ME FIND MY SON!!

Age: 6 years old

Race: Black, Brown complexion

Height: 4 ft 1 inch

Weight: 77 lbs

Hair: Black

Eyes: Brown

Wearing: blue baseball cap, white Negro League child jersey, green shorts and white gym shoes.

Last seen: 2 months ago, he was playing outside with friends at Arthur Ashe Beach Park on 74th & South Shore. He is very friendly but also autistic.

Please call (773) 555 – 7876

THERE'S NO REWARD. I HAVE NO MONEY!!!

PLEASE HELP ME! I WANT MY SON BACK!!!

GRAVEYARD BLUES

Oakwood Cemetery was not quiet tonight.

Situated in the middle of a Chicago south side neighborhood amid the usual sounds of revving car engines, trains in the distance, buses, and police sirens, there loomed this one hundred-sixty eight year old, 183 acre square of grass, hills and decorated stones. Partitioned away from public view by a near seven foot beige brick wall, the only thing taller were the trees within it and the occasional monument peeking over the top of it.

The gates of the entrance were large, elegant, green steel adorning the foreboding mystique that was the cemetery. The office had just closed for the evening and just beyond the gates, one vehicle slowly backed out of a parking space, making its way towards the exit.

As the car pulled out onto sixty-seventh street, on the other side walked a woman. She stepped into the grounds deliberately left foot first, turned back around and bent over to carefully place four pennies at the base on the right side of the gate. She then continued her walk down the middle of the pathway deeper into the cemetery. Just beyond the gates, were the peering eyes of some neighborhood men loosely following her, trying to get a good look at her backside.

One man, impressed by what he saw, opened his mouth to say something vile to get her attention. It's what they'd been doing all day while she walked through the neighborhood. Once he saw her walk defiantly into the garden of the dead, he fell silent, his heart pounding heavily for a few beats. He then turned and walked in the opposite direction.

She was oblivious to the collection of males outside the gates, instead her mind was on what she noticed upward. Half the sky was sunny with blue skies, the other half, the eastern half, was a gradual gray turning darker further east. It was hard to tell in which direction the clouds were moving. It was a front that somehow eluded the predictions of the weather forecasters and a sight that changed the plans of many people that unseasonably cool, summer Sunday afternoon. It seemed to change everyone's plans but hers.

Undaunted, she followed the concrete path as it curved to the right, passing towering obelisks and elaborate crypts. An occasional wind blew through her body, slightly lifting her jacket or moving a tuft of hair from her dark brown face. She closed her eyes and felt the cool wind caress her cheeks, almost blowing away the thoughts that brought her here this afternoon.

The sounds of the city started to fade and soon the sound of her footsteps on the pathway were the only thing piercing the growing silence. Memory brought her to a large section near the south wall of the grounds. There the sun began a game of hide and seek, slipping behind the clouds then reappearing, the effect had her walking in and out of moving shadows. One minute, taking in the warmth of the sun, then seconds later, the chill of the shade.

The sound of her heels on concrete gave way to the muffled sound of walking on grass; it was now a familiar section to her. She had been here before to lament and marvel at the history on the face of carved stones. It was the history of past

Chicago mayors like William Thompson and Harold Washington, lawyers like Cecil Parterre and Eugene Pincham. Olympians such as Jesse Owens and iconic businessmen like John H. Johnson.

The voices of her memory recited speeches from Mayor Harold Washington she learned at Nkrumah International Academy. Usually upon viewing these headstones, it felt as if the cemetery spoke to her, but not today. Today there was a different sound.

Just ahead, on her path, was a gaggle of geese several feet ahead. A large gander turned his head toward the visitor and took a step in her direction. A gentile warning that if she got too close, there may be trouble. She just smiled slightly, walking past without incident. The large bird proudly strutted back to his mate, having exerted his dominance. She marched on. Beyond the giant obelisks and crosses, there was the hill. That hill was her destination on this day.

Careful not to step on any flat headstones, she searched her mind for the right plot number, never paying attention to the subtle noises replacing the city sounds.

There! A few yards beyond her, she found the familiar name engraved upon a gray rectangular stone. *Granddad* her thoughts whisper.

She found it, immediately kneeling to clean rotted leaves, bugs and sticks from the face of the Bible shaped marker, the inscription becoming clear.

IN LOVING MEMORY
AUGUST WAKEFIELD
HUSBAND, FATHER, GRANDFATHER,
BORN AUGUST 22 1945 DIED DECEMBER 2----

Only the death date seemed to be worn away by time and the elements; she never thought to question why. She remembered when he died. In came the memories, some good, others not so good as she holds back the tears. It was the same reaction she experienced every time.

She reached back to her earliest memory of her grandfather. Her earliest image was of his warm smile. Christmas morning, as she raced with her siblings to the tree and dove into the multitude of toys spread out on the floor. She remembers looking up at the giant, lighted tree. The only thing taller was her granddaddy, whose smile was brighter than the lights on the decorated tree.

A smile formed on her face. She remembered, as a little girl, watching him work the crowd at their church where he was a deacon. Shaking hands and giving out hearty "God bless yous" to various people in the congregation. His smile warmed hearts and incited smiles in return.

She let out a sigh and tilted her head, a slight smile still present. When her father was sick and unable to drive her to school, who showed up with that smile to make the save and get her to her 4th grade class? Granddaddy. He even packed her an extra lunch, filled with her favorites so she could trade parts of her other lunch to raise her social standing with her classmates. So thoughtful he was. Tears welled up in her eyes.

She also remembered the night, while grand-mama was at choir practice, that granddaddy came into her room, telling her it was alright and touched her five year old body in places he'd never laid his hands before. She remembered the confusion, the fear, him moving her hand down the front his pants. He'd assured her their secret would be a special thing between them and that everything would be ok, all while he smiled his famous smile.

She remembered how her heart sank and her chest hurt, it was pumping so hard, just as it was as she sat by his grave. She also remembered when the money ran out for one of her semesters at college. When it looked like she would have to drop out, it was granddaddy who reached into his pension, without hesitation, and kept her in school. The entire family praised him and her mother was so relieved.

"Now you stay in there and get your degree. I will always love you...you're my special little girl." Those were the words her granddad told her as he handed her mother the check.

You're my special little girl... It reverberated through her being over and over again.

"I will always love you..." The unmistakably graveled voice of her granddad came from not inside her but from *beside* her. Her eyes caught him just a few yards away, casually leaning on a headstone. He looked healthy, unlike the last year of his life before the cancer withered him away. His button up sweater, loafers, beige khakis and even his gray Herringbone flat cap fit him perfectly. His eyes were clear and his face was full and healthy. Yet, she stared straight through him.

"I'm…I'm so happy you came to see me and I love you for that, but you have to go…" She kept staring.

"*Now* darling!" His ghostly presence emphasized as she wept. There was so much to say, too much. She should have taken heed.

Images from her life replayed behind her closed lids, all the memories came in a flood. She loved him, but she hated him more. She was afraid for her grandmother and the family. So to this very moment, she'd kept the darkness to herself. Maybe now her story could be told, maybe now she could finally relieve herself of a weight that had tormented her for years. A secret was in the grave. Would it rise up? Now sitting alone, she wanted to pray but she didn't know exactly what to pray for.

Before she could figure out what to say, she heard it. Then nothing. The city outside the gate was completely quiet. There was no sound except a rumble, barely audible. It was interrupted by silence then started again. A deep, subtle shake under her feet. She turned, tilting her head to listen more intently.

It was gone. Then it returned.

She placed her hand on the headstone to get her balance as she rose. Almost standing, she placed her hand again on the ground. Again this hum, this rumble vibrated in the earth. She was momentarily motionless in this position until a loud flutter of wings startled her from behind. She turned to see the geese flying away quickly.

"What's going on?" She whispered. After being still for a few seconds, the rumbling stopped. She bent over the grave to listen closely.

Nothing…

Suddenly, a heavy vibration moved from the earth through her body, shaking her to the core. She quickly turned to look behind her at the ground in amazement. The grass slowly swelled upward, forming a large hump. She gasped as the ground grew as if engorged with…something. Then it receded. It swelled again until a section of dirt cracked, then shrunk down again.

From within the cracked earth came a different, more terrifying sound, "Waaaahhhhrrr."

"The hell?!" This time there was no whisper but a shout erupting from her shock as she whirled her head around to what she thought was the source of the sound, her eyes wide open. She bent down again, placed her ear to the ground, only to hear silence.

Silence…

Then, out of nowhere, there was a voice, muffled by layers of dirt; it sounded like a man screaming. She jumped, mouth open and stared at the site where her head had just rested. The vibration returned harder and louder. The hum…it…it was the sound of voices, of screaming voices. Her ears picked up more moaning, ever so low, but near her. The earth below her feet vibrated out of rhythm, sending panic through her legs. She stood up completely, taking a step back only to be met by more moans and screams surrounding her in every direction. They were low, subtle, but in the deathly stillness of the graveyard, they may as well have been car alarms or sirens.

With a scared heart pounding, the woman took more steps away from her grandfather's grave, a confused and frightened look on her face. The vibrations flowed in waves with each step, the hums now screams echoing throughout the cemetery. She hadn't noticed the sky turning completely dark as storm clouds rushed in with no rain. The sudden drop in temperature sent a cold chill throughout her entire core.

As she continued slowly backing away from the grave, out the corner of her eye, she saw a huge, square tombstone suddenly fall forward, impacting the ground with a muffled thud. Instinctively, she turned toward it

NO! RUN!!! her inner voice demanded. Keeping an eye on the fallen tombstone and her ears on the ever increasing screams and moans emanating around her, she started her escape from the damned cemetery. She picked up her pace on the pathway leading back to the entrance gate. Racing pass the grave sites of mayors, Olympic gold medalists, Confederate soldiers, gangsters, scientists, all of whose tombstones began to shake violently as she passed. Her speed walk became a jog down the middle of the concrete as she urgently made her way to the gates, never turning her head to witness what would undoubtedly scare the hell out of her.

The front of the cemetery was in sight! She could see the beautiful stone opening, but with each step, the gates appeared to slowly swing closer, as if attempting to trap her in. A panic rose in the woman's chest, as her jog became a full on run toward the once beautiful gates now betraying her.

Avoiding the pointy edges and stumbling over cracks in the concrete, she quickly dashed through the gates that were indeed closing. As a last attempt to entrap her, the lock on the gate seemed to reach out, grabbing the arm of her lightweight jacket. In an act of pure desperation, she shrugged out of it, leaving it ensnared on the metal. The gates slammed shut with

what almost sounded like an angry growl when her feet hit the
sidewalk.

Standing outside the grounds of the cemetery, she looked
back inside. The graves beyond the gates seemed to change color
under the overcast sky. For her, there was no sound on the street,
even though cars were passing by. She only heard the screams
and echoes of tortured moans still resonating in her ears. She
spoke quietly to herself as she rushed home.

"The cemetery is alive."

FX NOZAKHERE

HAPPY ANNIVERSARY

He woke up suddenly from his nap, with a shake of his head and squint of his eyes, he looked over to the LED clock on the wall. It was 8:03pm. He jumped up, smoothed out his white shirt, straightened his collar and pressed the wrinkles in his black slacks with his hands.

"Did I miss her or is she just late?" he asked the empty room while shuffling to put on his black dress shoes.

"God, I hope I didn't miss her at the door." His eyes reflected a worry that caused his heart to pump in his stomach. He immediately jogged a short distance to the front window and peered out into the evening darkness. His eyes perused the black for any sign of anyone familiar.

Finding nothing but darkness, he turned from the window, hastily walking to the kitchen. He flung open the refrigerator and grabbed the nearest bottle of grape juice. It was out of nervousness, and a small fear, that he drank, not thirst. He was trying to keep his mouth from becoming dry, a sure sign of overactive nerves. It was a nervousness that rose as he looked towards the crack in the blinds and saw a light move across the window.

"Is that her in the driveway?" Now excitement, along with that fear, enraptured him, energizing him to move quickly towards the front door. He paused for a second, placed the bottle down on a nearby table and looked through the peephole, a subtle smile brightening his face.

David Wesley opened the door and there she stood, greeting him with an immediate smile, her caramel-colored face glowing with the warmth of loving recognition, she even snickered slightly.

"Hello David." Her voice was a welcomed sound in his ears and upon his heart. His smile now widening with a nervous anticipation.

"You made it...get in here beautiful." His nervousness amused her.

Sharon Attah floated in with the grace of a ballerina, her

white dashiki billowed and flowed gracefully behind her. Her straight black hair flowed with her gown and with just as much elegance. David watched her every move with amazement. Still nervous, he turned to take a quick look outside the door then closed and locked it. He turned to her and found her looking at him smiling. He started towards her with his arms outstretched but stopped, lowering them. She chuckled at his awkwardness.

"How was your...trip over here?" he asked.

"I had no problems. I can get here so fast now, it seems." She answered. His excitement was hard to hide as he motioned her to the living room area "You know you're at home...come rest yourself."

"Why do you act so nervous around me David?" she asked with a slight Nigerian accent while making her way to her favorite brown recliner. She tucked her dress under her and slowly sat down, awaiting his answer. David's eyes never strayed from her, his nervousness slowly subsiding.

"I'm not nervous..." he finally answered, while moving to

sit on the couch across from Sharon.

"Bullsheet! Yes you are! It's cute but we are wayyyy past that now David. So stop acting new...you knew I was coming ova and I would not miss seeing you." Sharon laughingly retorted.

"I'm just happy to see you, it's been... a while," David said shyly.

"A year David..." Sharon interjected with a smile.

He shook his head in the affirmative, "Yes, a year...I'm just...happy anniversary Sharon." Sharon continued to smile, just staring at David before she answered.

"Yes, happy anniversary my love."

They stopped and stared into each other's eyes as if they were teenagers in love, the time apart didn't matter at this moment. The relief in his eyes connected with the light in hers. He fidgeted like a child, she caressed her hair like a supermodel.

"So, tell me..." Sharon readjusted herself in the recliner, ready to hear David's account, "...how is the new school?" David immediately snapped out of his stare.

"Oh, yeah…it's…I like Chicago State, it's going good. The students are actually eager to learn. There are even a few prospects that seem to have a knack, a natural inclination for science and…and chemistry."

"Like the students in Kaduna? Remember them?" said Sharon. David smiled.

"Yesssss, haha, like the students in Kaduna. I know where you're going with that…don't start." His playful retort was cute to Sharon.

"And I stand by it…" Sharon replied.

"You can stand by it but that still doesn't mean these kids in America aren't hungry for knowledge." David proudly stated.

"But you know it David, the students in Naija, even all of Africa, are more hungry, more passionate for learning, for education…" Her hands motioned to express her point.

"But, you know what about my students?" David interrupted.

"What?"

DuSable City

"It's the female students, it's mostly the…"

"You're a chemist David, not a zoologist. Women, not females." Sharon laughed.

"My bad! You're right, the women. The women students are mostly the ones showing a lot of excitement and proficiency in a subject matter that most educators and sociologists over the years have said was a weak point for women."

David's eyes lit up when he talked of his students. He loved his job, especially now that he'd made the change to Chicago State University from the University of Illinois in Chicago.

"I have huge plans for those students, all of them, and the school. We're going to put Chicago State on the map." Sharon was always proud of him, even amazed by his mental prowess and aspirations which made her want to support him as he supported her.

"Those students are fortunate to have you as a teacher, but how is your theoretical research going?"

"That's the thing Sharon, I'm going to float it to the students, I'm going to let them expand my theories. Of course I'll coach them, but I need to give them their own space to see if they come to the same conclusions I came to...I think they will." David was visibly excited like the young students he was talking about.

"Oh ok, that's a great idea." Sharon's eyes widened at David's ideas.

"The core principles in my research can be planted in young fertile minds. This could be the way of the future for this university...." David's hand pointed in the air as if highlighting every word. "...that's the line I told the school president that won her over."

"With your brilliant bad ass! Look at you!" Sharon turned her head and finished her praise of David with a laugh.

"Thank you baby. You are too kind!" David was almost blushing through his brown skin. He stood up and walked over to the table where he placed the bottle of sparkling grape.

Returning to the couch, he picked up the remote to the DVD player, hit a series of buttons and soon the deep bass of Frankie Beverly and Maze flowed from the speakers.

"Happy feelings in the aaaaaaaaiiirrrr...touching people everywheeeeeeeerrrre..."

Sharon's face lit up as she turned toward the music, "I love that song David!" She turned back to him with one eye brow raised and a sly, almost seductive smile.

"What you trying..." David took two wine glasses and poured one drink, paused and poured another, "....to do?"

She watched him and her countenance changed, pausing first at the glasses then she looked up at him.

David noticed her seeming hesitation, "I know, it's out of re..."

"It's ok..." she interrupted, closing her eyes as her smile returned. "You're still not drinking?" She asked.

"No I'm not. Done with it," a serious tone lacing his words.

"That's good love. I'm proud of you." Sharon was happy for his staunch, self- imposed discipline because she knew it did not come easy.

"How long now?" she asked. David raised his glass to his lips, he took his first sip then quietly said..

"Three years." She acknowledged his words with a shake of her as he sipped the contents of his glass.

The music filled the space between them, serenading them into the night as they delved deep into conversation that covered a multitude of topics. Whether or not Chicago State University could be considered an HCBU, Chicago politics and the real world chemistry applications to Mary Shelly's Frankenstein. The musical accompaniments to their conversation including Earth Wind and Fire, Stevie Wonder and Angela Winbush.

Hours pass.

"...And, the look on Professor Petrov's face when I told him I was uhhh...leaving for CSU...." David continued, now sitting on the floor and leaning against the couch.

"He was proud but surprised you actually did it." Sharon added.

"Exactly how he looked Sharon...exactly." David validated her point as he took another sip from a recently refilled glass of sparkling grape.

"He's a good guy...never gave me the headaches the rest of the board did." He continued between sips.

"But I think they were still kind of...proud, if I can say that, of you being there David." Sharon said.

"Yes, but I had to do what I needed to do. I had a vision, we both did. I wanted my vision fulfilled with you and your law career at..." David halted his statement, he even paused his movements. He slowly peered up at Sharon who was still smiling and about to speak.

"I remember your..." She too paused, her smile frozen but it no longer had meaning. "I remember your..." her smile melted away, "...David?" She turned her head as if to survey her surroundings.

David slowly put down his wine glass, keeping his eyes on her; readying himself.

Her smile returned, "I was...where is the law firm? Was I...I was in the woods walking but the car had stalled on us?" Her eyes stared off into nothing, her hand was still in mid-air as if she was reaching for something.

"David?" She whispered.

He slowly rose from the floor, "Sharon..." he whispered, "...stay with me, here." His voice had become urgent.

The music stopped.

Sharon twisted her body to view everything around her, even looking up towards the ceiling.

"No David....no, no, noooo." Panic snaked into her voice.

"Baby, look at me! I'm right here! I haven't gone anywhere!" The panic in David's voice rose to match hers. "I'm right he...."

"David!" She shot up out of the recliner, her hands grasping her temples, her eyes tightly closed as she continued to yell out what her mind was seeing.

"David, the....there's blood! I saw blood! My home...my faaather! I was just...where is...I was just downtown at the..."

David stood, watching Sharon's actions, frightened at what may come next. He forcibly calmed himself in an attempt to calm her.

"Sharon, look at me baby. Listen to me...you're alright. Everything is ok baby. Please look at me!" His voice was filled with desperation.

Sharon suddenly went silently, her arms flopping down by her sides and turned her back to David. Seconds pass but to David it felt like hours.

"No, it isn't David." His eyes widened, mouth opened but no sound came out.

"This is not alright...this is not all right. You David..."

David's heart sunk at the accusatory tone in his loves' voice.

Sharon finally turned towards him, "Damn you David."

She declared, her voiced seething.

"No Sharon, I'm...here, keep yourself together, don't go off, please! Sharon just stay here with me..."

"No, you should not be. How many times David?! How many times must we, must I do this?!

"Sharon calm down please!"

"NO DAVID, I WILL NOT CALM DOWN!!!" Sharon's face contorted into anger, her hands became fists, her smile a grim frown, the glow from her eyes dimmed into darkness, penetrating his very soul.

"This...THIS is not happening to you David!" She screamed.

The scream snapped David out of his panic, "No, this *is* happening to me! It happened to both of us! I'm just trying to make a bad situation better for...."

"You've made it worse David, you don't see that? Every year for the past three years...and...and last time I knew then! And that affects me David, do you not see that?!" Sharon's voice echoed through David's apartment,; the wine glasses shook.

"Ok, ok, what can I do to make you relax?! I need you to calm down Sharon. You're going to hurt…"

Sharon shot back "I'm already hurt David! *YOU'RE* already hurt!" Sharon took two steps toward David, fear grasped David's heart and he stepped back.

"Sharon." She immediately stopped, looking at David hard, finally seeing his reaction to her. Her eyes widened then narrowed, her face settled into an angry calm.

"Da…David…I'm sorry, I didn't mean to scare you." Her voice lowered. "This isn't me, this is you." she added.

David, while relieved at her growing calm, concentrated on words that would keep her that way.

"I just wanted to make you feel better, an evening together for our anniversary. I didn't think it would be any harm…I…just wanted to make things right, for you." His voice pleaded with her.

"You don't know…you don't know what you've done, what you're doing David…" she stepped closer to him, this time with softness. She raised her hand as if to caress his cheek but stopped short. He didn't flinch this time.

"Things are not right, they haven't been since…the accident. David my love…" David brow furrowed.

"I know, it was my fault!" He whimpered, a completely broken sound.

"No, no it wasn't!" Sharon responded.

"Yes." He whispered, defeated.

"No David, but this…" She waved her hand to encompass the entire apartment, "…this is. This is not right and this *is* your fault. You have to know that…you're hurting me."

"I'm a scientist, I don't understand this! This is unprecedented! It's never happened to me before, to anybody!" David finally broke down.

He had reached a level of knowledge that few have ever achieved. The praise, the accolades, even the jealous colleagues weren't enough to curtail the agony of facing this place in time. His tears came fast, this was the heaviest moment between them in three years.

"Where is it David?" Sharon calmly asked. Sobbing, David collapsed on the couch, not willing to face her and the question she'd just asked. It was just too devastating.

"You can fix this David." Suddenly, he felt the absence of her presence. He opened his eyes, hoping to see her, yet knowing she was gone.

Slowly he rose to his feet. His mouth open, tears already drying on his cheeks, he called out to her, turning his head slowly to scan the room. He wiped his eyes and cheeks, and slowly walked through his home.

"Sharon? Where did you go?" he cautiously called out for her. "I don't...I don't like it when you do this."

He felt a heaviness overcome him, the sound was sucked out of the apartment but he could once again feel her presence.

"Sharon?" He stopped, closed his eyes and felt for her, extending his spirit to try to contact hers.

Feeling around for Sharon, using only his love, he found

her, where he should have known she'd be.

Opening his eyes, he turned slowly toward the back room and started a slow walk to the closed door at the end of the dimly lit hall. Every step brought a heavier pounding of his heart, as if a hammer was in his chest.

"Why am I scared?" he asked himself, never bothering to answer.

While mentally replaying the words of his love, David could feel the vibe of her presence get heavier the closer he got to the door. With every creak of the old wood, he could hear a sound emanating from behind the closed door. Just on the other side, he could hear subtle sighs, then, a voice. It was feminine and undeniable.

He reached for the doorknob and slowly turned. With a click, the locks gave way and he gently pushed the door open, stepping into darkness and uncertainty. The bedroom windows provided light from the streetlamps which helped illuminated parts of the unlit room. Everything was in place; chair, desk, lamp as his eyes scanned the area of the bed... it was there. In the air

was the pungent odor of chemicals, incense and perfume; all of it

together, making a strange new smell.

He stepped further in, hands down to his side and shaking

just a bit. Still looking through the room, his eyes settled on what

was an unusually dark figure just a few feet to his right. It did not

move. Instead, he moved toward it.

He had a desire to speak but not one word left his mouth.

Instead, the dark figure spoke.

"David..." her sweet voice took on a more ethereal sound

and it calmed him, "...my love, you have to stop. You have to

come back from where you are that did this...this is what I mean,

and you know it, don't you?"

Without saying anything, his eyes veered away from her,

his head lowered just a little as if shamed by something deep

within him. He turned towards the side of the bed, reached up to

the light switch on the wall and flipped it.

A white bulb flooded the room with brilliance. The white

walls beamed with reflective light, causing him to squint. She remained unmoved, the sudden light revealed her staring directly at what lie on the bed.

It was half covered by a pristine white blanket which contrasted harshly against the dingy, graying dashiki. The brown sunken face and head stood out boldly against the white. The arms rested across the abdomen, over the blanket, with the hands crossed right over left. The skin of the hands was smooth with not a wrinkle was present. The fingers were stuck in a permanent outstretched position. The still gleaming hair blended perfectly into the highly polished dark brown headboard.

Her once beautiful face was swollen slightly, mouth shut, eyes closed and denying him the light that once emanated from them. The pillow holding the head was flattened in the middle by its weight, the ends fluffed forward almost obscuring the face from the side. The upward protruding lumps at the foot of the bed gave away the length. This was a testament to a growing pain, overflowing yet bound with rationalizations.

"One night a year, I couldn't just do that. I...I needed

to…" his voice cracked as he sputtered to speak through his pain.

She interrupted. "You have to get rid of this! Bury it, bury me…my remains. I cannot go on until you do. I am tied to it and this is unnatural."

David sheepishly replied "If you're still…tied to it then we can still be together." She finally took her eyes away from her dead body to look at him. Her face a mix of emotions. David turned towards the specter of Sharon and continued,

"You can still come visit me…" She slowly shook her head in the negative, her eyes rolled upward and her mouth frowned.

"I don't want you to leave me." His voice cracked again.

"Dammit, you're being selfish even now! You've always been selfish, but this is fucking ridiculous. Your guilt and selfishness are keeping me trapped here…" She shot back, her voice rising and much more adamant.

His eyes widened as his hands raised to calm her, but she was unresponsive to his gesture.

"You have to let go! You have to let your guilt go! Dammit! The accident wasn't your fault my love...you can come back from the edge, set me free and you'll be setting us both free. Bury this thing, bury me and let me go. I will always be with you in your memories, in your heart and you will still be in mine. Please, I can't do this anymore, I DON'T WANT TO!!"

"Sharon..." he pleaded, "...I'm in hell and I've been suffering since you died. I couldn't lose you then and I can't lose you now. We had just gotten married and I ruined it but now I've made it so you can stay with me forever. All I have to do is keep you from...falling apart, I figured out how."

"Babe, you're trying to keep me from falling apart but it's you that's falling apart. You've been falling apart! This..." she spread her hands toward the body on the bed.

"...This will continue to decay because it's not me anymore. Your science can't undo death. You're just endangering yourself...some type of germs or the police will catch up with you or someone will figure out what the weird smell is. Love, you will be found out and this shit will go horribly wrong."

DuSable City

David folded his arms, resting his right arm on his left, his hand covering his face while his fingers rubbed his temples.

"Love, every year for the past 3 years, it's the same shit. You're stressing me out and I can't keep myself together when I'm stressed, when I'm angry. I'm going to disappear again and loop right back here, again, to have the same conversation. You don't know what I'm going through, my existence or lack of it. I don't want this, I can't do this anymore. You have to let me go if you love me!

He lifted his head from his hands, his arms dropped to the side. "I do love you." It came out in a wounded sob.

"Then let me go. Let me die." Her voice pleaded in that soft, persuasive way that had always melted him.

He stood with his head lowered. She hovered staring at him, awaiting for his response. There was quiet between them until the loudest noise came from what was on the bed.

Sharon spoke almost a whisper "Let your guilt die. Bury me and set us both free." He lifted his tear streaked face to hers, hoping to find comfort in her loving eyes, but she was gone.

Realizing he was alone, his sobs grew louder until he almost hyperventilated. He stepped back to the wall, sliding to the floor, his face a mask of grief. She was dying all over again, right before his eyes and he could do nothing to stop it...again.

He sat at the base of the wall like a child on punishment, his cries calming just enough to say, "God help me...what have I done?!"

An hour later.

No one noticed a lone SUV driving down the near empty street at 3:15 in the morning. No one noticed it turn right onto 67th street and slowly proceed toward the graveyard entrance. No one saw the man get out and somehow unlock the chain around the gates. No one noticed the gates of the cemetery swing open and the SUV drive through.

No one witnessed the man shoveling silently for well over an hour, or carrying a body wrapped in a white pristine blanket and placing it in the newly dug grave.

DuSable City

The next morning, the sun beams rays of bright light into the apartment, signaling a new day. A table for two is still set in the dining area. Two wine glasses are still on the living room table, one empty, the other filled with sparkling grape juice. In a bedroom, beyond an open door, is an empty bed with nothing more than a mattress resting upon it.

On the couch lay Dr. David Wesley, still wearing his clothes from the previous day, sullied with dirt and grass. He has passed out from sheer exhaustion with tears stains streaking his face.

Suddenly, an almost transparent hand begins to caress his low afro, then his tear-streaked cheek. The cold, prickly feel of her ethereal touch makes him stir in his sleep. The woman bends to silently embrace him.

"Thank you my love. I will always be with you." She says ever so softly, then kisses his forehead. She stands and walks out the front door, never opening it.

Dr. David Wesley smiles deeply in his sleep as the sun's

FX NOZAKHERE

warming rays touch his face and begin to melt away the grief surrounding his once tortured heart. They were both now free to move on...

THE JENKINS FAMILY

"Deshawn! Go take yo' sistah ha food!" Deshawn's heart suddenly weighed fifty pounds heavier, his mother's voice echoed in his limbs and he began to shake.

Sitting in the middle of the floor in his room, surrounded by school books, he rose to his feet and carefully stepped over the mass of pencils, erasers, notebooks and textbooks. He turned his husky body to the door and stopped, taking in a long breath with his eyes closed, as he proceeded to the door, slowly opened it and walked out his room.

"Deshawn! Boy you hear me callin' you?!" His mother's voice boomed through the house.

"Yes mama." Deshawn responded with his usual low toned voice. He turned the corner into the sunlit living room. His shoulders were hunched slightly making his red Michael Jordan t-shirt look larger than it was. The boy's eyes widened as if he was in a constant state of apprehension or fear.

Deshawn walked his sock covered feet across the matted

gray carpet to his mother's side. The light from the windows revealed a recently straightened up area, it was the effort of his mother and him cleaning and straightening up in preparation of the visitor sitting before them. Yet, it was still an obviously lived in space, with cups on the table, newspapers strewn about the furniture and walls that needed dusting. Deshawn never understood why his mother simultaneously reviled these visits yet cleaned up the house in order to impress those she hated. *It must be to make them think we alright people,* he thought to himself.

"C'mere boy," his mother stretched her dark arm out towards Deshawn, her underarm fat shook as it dangled. Deshawn stood to his mother's side resting his hand on the arm of her chair. He was trying his best not to show on the outside what he felt on the inside. *Best face forward,* he thought.

"Dis cheer my youngest boy, Deshawn, buh you aw'ready know dat, dontcha'?" His mother rubbed his afro with her right hand. "He mah' right hand man, whaeva I need dun, he do." Her smile was one of genuine pride.

"Hello Deshawn, nice to meet you. Ok, I'm ready...so

now we can get on with the interview," said the white woman sitting across from his mother. "Now I have De....Dee...Shawn?"

"Deshawn. Just like ah jus' said a few seconds ago." His mother shot back.

"Deshawn, thank you. Now Ms. Jenkins..." she wiped a strand of hair from her forehead, "...can you spell your name for me?"

Dressed in a beige pantsuit with white pearls hanging from her neck, the white woman scribbled onto her notepad then began shuffling papers until one fell on the floor.

"Deshawn, go get yo' sistah ha food, now boy." She gently yet carelessly mushed Deshawn on the side of his head as she stared directly at the white woman who was totally oblivious to her stare and her dropped papers.

Deshawn caught eye of the fallen pieces, he turned to his mother then looked to the case worker. He stepped towards her side and picked up the paper, "You dropped dis."

He didn't look at her, instead, he caught a glimpse of the

header on one of the papers as he handed it to the woman.

Deshawn had wondered when the day would come when the city

would come to actually take them away from his mother. He felt

like this may be the day as he read "**The Department of**

Children and Family Services" on the paper.

"Oh, thank you young man, I'm so clumsy today, I don't

know why…" she said.

"Umm hmm! 'Cause you a white woman in Englewood

bout to ask me questions about my family, and it's Yolanda…" the

mother shot back again.

Nervously the case worker replied to the charge,

"I'm….I'm just…I want to make sure you and your family are

alright, it's my job. Yola…." She fumbled with her pen.

"Y - O, Yo!" the mother never took her eyes off the DCFS

case worker.

"Ok, y – o…" the case worker followed up, "Landa', l – a

– n – d….." the mother took a long pause, "….a."

"Yo….landa, and I have Jenkins, ok thank you." The case

worker made sure to accent her voice with courtesy, the effort
was obvious

Yolanda Jenkins sat on the end of the couch barely hiding
her exasperation at what was sitting across the table from her. She
straightened out her long Afrikaan print skirt, pulled a piece of
lint from her blue tank top and patted her long hair to relieve an
itch. She looked across the living room to watch her son Deshawn
enter the kitchen to make sure he found the food for her daughter.

After watching him grab the correct bag she focused her
attention on the woman in front of her. *Again with these
muthafuckas* she thought to herself, shaking her head slightly,
while the DCFS case worker fiddled with her papers. She may
have been talking to her but Yolanda wasn't listening. She was
keeping a seething part of her in control. *This bland pantsuit
wearing...*

"Who fuc....did yo' hair?" Yolanda asked. A puzzled look
came over the case workers face.

"Excuse me?"

"Yo' hair, it looks so fascinatin'." She did little to hide her belittling sarcasm.

"Ms. Jenkins, I don't understand why you're giving me such a hard time. I mean, I really don't know. I can't tell if you're joking with me for levity's sake or just being uncooperative, and if it's the latter, please ma'am, I'm just here to help. The agency is here to help you. Now, your son Deshawn he...is not..." she ruffled her papers searching for the information. Her head was lowered as she intensely scanned her paperwork.

Yolanda gave no answer, instead she stared just beyond the case worker where her twin sons stood. One, extremely dark-skinned and dressed in all black with a long black coat. The other, the albino, was dressed in all white with a long white coat. The albino held a bloodied machete over the head of the caseworker. The son in all black looked to his mother for a sign. Yolanda shook her head "no" casually.

The case worker finally organized her question, "You have two more boys, other than Deshawn correct? Twins I understand George and William?"

"Yea." Yolanda responded curtly. Her eyes fixated on the subjects behind the case worker. The white lady looked up from her notes, asking.

"And how are they, Ms. Jenkins?"

Still staring behind the woman, Yolanda responded, "Oh...they are fine." The case worker saw that she looked past her.

"What's wrong?" She asked, immediately turning to see what was behind her. There was nothing, just more empty room. Yolanda smirked and let out a chuckle.

Unnerved the case worker turned back to the mother slowly, "Ahem'" and went back to her notes.

"I see. George and William, where are th..."

Yolanda interrupted, "I sent them out to get food and to visit...a friend." She sat forward and began shuffling small bottles on the living room table between her and her visitor.

"And your daughter Ayesha? Is she home?"

"Mah lil' angel is tied up right now."

"In her room?" The case worker asked innocently.

"In da basement, she like goin' down there but lately she got a lil' sick, a lil' col' virus." Yolanda explained as she pulled a small weighted tea bag from one of the containers. The case worker nodded her head in understanding, never paying attention to what Yolanda was doing.

"I see. So, she's doing alright then?"

"Yea, she fine, or she will be. I jus sent ha brutha to take ha some food. I let dem play down there and to keep her busy while I'm busy wid you."

"Oh ok. very well. In what way do you discipline your children Ms. Jenkins? Do you spank them? Put them in time-out? Take away their privileges? Lecture them?" The case worker kept her head in the paperwork on her lap to await an answer.

"I use ta' knock the shit out of 'em..." Yolanda started. The case worker's head shot up and she looked totally shocked. Yolanda waited for that response and continued "...but ah stopped that cuz of things like this shit here." The case worker's brows furrowed at what she heard, her mouth opened as if to speak but Yolanda continued again. "And it hurt them too much. I got sum badass kids but..." she paused, "...I don't want to see them hurt."

Her cadence slowed and softened, "They was hurt enuff when they gran'mama died."

"Yes, you have my condolences on the passing of your mother, so sad." The lack of sincerity in the caseworker's voice almost made Yolanda jump off the couch.

"Yeah...thank you," the words were dripping with the same level of insincerity. There was an awkward silence as the case worker scribbled notes. Yolanda was deep in thought as she continued toying the items on the table. She handled a small bag the contents of which weighed it down.

She sat back as if to relax and in the process, raised her left knee to place her foot on the couch. Her skirt raised just enough to reveal a panty-less glimpse of her womanhood. The eyes of the DCFS worker caught that glimpse and held it for two seconds. She then looked up to see Yolanda smirking and staring right into her eyes with brief curiosity.

"You a lesbian Ms. whats-your-face?" Yolanda asked, attempting to stifle the laughter in her voice. The case worker turned her gaze away and straightened out some papers, she looked back as if shocked.

"Excuse me Ms. Jenkins?"

"Is you a lesbian? I mean, did something catch yo' eye?" Yolanda's raised eyebrow was accompanied by a sly smirk.

Nervously, the case worker replied, "Ms Jenkins please. That is highly inappropriate for this..."

"Bitch, I'm jus playin' wid choo!" Yolanda let out a hearty laugh while waving her hands. The case worker regained her composure wiping away a few strands of brown hair and tucking it behind her right ear.

"Now Ms. Jenkins...uhm Yolanda, I'm not sure you understand the gravity of this situation, of why I'm here." Her voice regained some of its authoritative tone. Never had she ever been given such a hard time during an investigative visit. Not in all her time as a DCFS case worker. Barbara Kanady had been yelled at, threatened, had parents cry on her shoulder and did her part to carry children away from homes while at other times, she found satisfaction in reuniting children with their parents or finding children new homes. But there was something about this case, this mother, this family, *these* people, that unnerved her.

"If I may say so Ms. Jenkins, I am just doing what I can to ensure the health and safety of your children. This is what the **Department of Children and Family Services** wants for you. I am not here to disrespect you or break up your family. Hopefully you don't think that. I, we, only want what's best for you. At the same time I am not here to be disrespected, so please work with me. The racial statement you made, asserting my sexual orientation, unnecessary. I want to help this family. I want to save this family as best I can, so please help me help you."

Yolanda stared at the case worker and smirked, "*You* are gonna save *my* family?"

"You have at risk children in one of the most dangerous

neighborhoods in Chicago and quite frankly, the history of your family and the tragedies you've gone through, how has this affected your chil..."

"Would you like some tea Ms. Kanady?" Yolanda interrupted politely.

"Huh? Excuse me? Tea?" the woman expressed a sudden confusion at being stopped in mid-sentence with an odd and politely asked question.

Yolanda wound up and threw her arm toward the case worker as gray powder flew from her hand, most of it landing in Ms. Kanady's face. She immediately screamed and turned her head away, her arms went up to protect her face, her briefcase and paperwork spilled onto the floor.

Happening at the same time in another part of the house, Deshawn timidly opened the basement door and his was engulfed in darkness. The stale air immediately assaulted his nostrils and he recoiled. Carefully gripping the bag, he descended the first step, then the second. As his eyes adjusted to the dark just enough to make out the stair railing, there was a shuffling sound on the floor below. The third step, then the fourth. He heard metal jingling. The fifth step, the sixth. The further he descended, the further his heart dropped. The seventh step, eighth.

"DEEEesssssSShhhaaaaawWWnnN....nanana."

Deshawn stopped, contemplating dropping the bag and running back upstairs. The sound of his name whispered like that shook him. It was a harsh reminder of what he was about to encounter.

He finally moved to the ninth step, then the tenth. A girl giggled softly, another sound of metal scraping the stone floor. Deshawn could now fully make out the bottom of the basement, most importantly, the light switch on the wall to the right. He paused then took the final three steps.

Eleventh, twelfth, thirteenth, hit the switch quickly. A dim, yellowish light flickered on and a small portion of the basement was now completely visible. The light was blocked by boxes and pillars, creating shadows throughout the area. Deshawn was ready to see what he knew was there but *there* was nothing, just boxes and space. He nervously looked around, eyes wide and darting, scanning the basement for his sibling.

The largest shadow was at the back of the basement, where the sounds were coming from. It was there that two yellowish eyes shone through the dark, looking directly at him.

"Ahh, my brother, what have you for me?" the voice was masculine but distorted and gravely. Deshawn held his head down and away from the eyes peering at him, he didn't want to see; he never wanted to see. His grip on the bag lightened, he was ready to put it down. "I brought....you sum' f..food."

"Oh, thank you my brother...that is sssoo sweet of you." The eyes in the shadows moved slightly with every word. Then they blinked.

Deshawn bent down to place the bag on the floor, readying his legs into a running position.

"Now Deshawn, you know damn well I cannot reach that!" The eyes said.

Deshawn almost started to cry. "It's right here," his voice shook as he laid the bag on the floor, his eyes finally looking up into the shadow ahead.

"Bring it to me..." Deshawn shook his head no.

"Bring it to me...come closer." The eyes demanded. Deshawn hesitated before he grabbed the bag and held it close to his chest. He gripped it as if it was his only line of defense.

"I promise I won't hurt you." The voice changed to the calming voice of a girl, soft and vulnerable. Deshawn stood still, he recognized the voice but it still sent waves of fear through his frozen legs. He leaned forward as if to proceed, but then leaned back, as if he'd changed his mind.

"Deshawn, you're my brother, I would never hurt you." The eyes swayed to the left as they talked. "I'm in chains, I cannot possibly hurt you even if I wanted to..."

Breaking through his fear, Deshawn managed to utter "The last time I came down here you..."

"...The chains are hurting me." She, it whimpered.

Deshawn continued, "...you scared me. You scarin' me now!"

"I'm the one locked away in a basement, bound in chains and you're scared?!" The voice grew more insistent.

Deshawn whimpered out a frail "Yea." There was no reply from the eyes, they just continued to stare right at the boy. There was a creaking sound, as if bones and joints were popping. The eyes suddenly began to rise upward, up, up until they were near the ceiling. Deshawn, now terrified, screamed "mama!" but he was so filled with terror he couldn't tell if he'd screamed it, or just thought it. The eyes, seemingly reacting to his scream, lowered, sounds of cracking and skin stretching could still be heard. Still, the eyes returned to their original size, slowly turning clockwise, upside down, around, then back to their original position.

Deshawn dropped the bag. "Here, take it!" Sprinting towards the stairs.

"No, I can't reach it! Deshawn! Deshawn! Imma' teeeell

mama!" This time it was a voice he remembered that stopped him in his escape. He looked back, terrified and confused, a tear forming in the corner of his right eye.

"What are you?! What's wrong with you?!" He raised his voice momentary in pure frustration. The voice that haunted him coupled with the voice of joyful recognition wracked his young, eleven year old mind.

"I'm sick...you know I'm sick. Mama keeps me down here because..." the voice from the eyes softened as if to look for mercy.

"Because you hurt people!" Deshawn quickly responded then turned to run up the stairs.

"Do you remember when you held me? Deshawn?" The boy stopped, the combination of her voice and a memory he cherished nearly caused another tear to form.

"When I was just a little baby? It was Christmas, I was under the tree with mama and you came over with the bottle of milk mama asked you to get off the table. Do you remember that?" the eyes said.

Deshawn took a step backwards off the stairs, he turned his head to the shadow and fixed his eyes on *those* eyes.

"Mama said 'you wanna' feed her?' and you said…"

"Yes." Deshawn quietly responded.

"Yeessss! Mama gave my tiny lil' self to you, you weren't much bigger than me but you struggled for a bit and held me…and fed me my bottle. I just looked up at you. The first time I looked up at my big brother, I knew then that I loved you so." the eyes seemingly softened. "Deshawn, I could never hurt you, especially not you, my big brother."

By now the boy was completely off the steps, standing in the light, he wiped his brow of the fear induced sweat he'd accumulated. He looked directly at the eyes, they looked directly at him. It was quiet. The eyes blinked, making a sound. Testament to just how quiet it now was.

Deshawn calmed down enough to feel the stale air again. He looked down at the bag he'd dropped, mustered up some courage and walked to the bag, slowly picking it up then looking

to see where the eyes were. They were right there, still staring at

him. He straightened and took a step towards the shadows.

Then another. The eyes widened.

He proceeded to take another step. The eyes grew wider.

He took his final step to stop in front of the shadow and slowly

knelt, never taking his eyes off *those* eyes. They suddenly moved

towards him, a scraping sound accompanied them.

By now Deshawn and the eyes were close, so close he

could hear breathing which was more like wheezing. He was

close enough to the eyes that he could see white teeth form in the

darkness. He hadn't seen her face in a week, so he looked to see if

she was still familiar, if she was still related to him, if it was still

her.

An arm stretched from the darkness and grabbed

Deshawn's wrist. He jumped, trying to yank his body away but to

no avail, a large clawed hand had a full grasp on him.

Deshawn screamed and fell to the basement floor, he

shuffled his feet to try to get away but the large hand tightened as he whimpered and closed his eyes. He didn't want to see it, he didn't want to see what his sister had become. And the eyes, they hovered just in front of him, seemingly unconcerned with his fear.

As they narrowed to tiny slits, a low growl erupted from the eyes without a face. Deshawn tried to yell for his mother but he stopped short, remembering the DCFS worker upstairs and thinking this might be the very thing that breaks up the family, but at the risk of his own life?

He looked back at his hand, expecting to see the horrifying claw tearing at his skin. Instead, it was the little brown hand of a girl. Without a word, she let him go. He snatched his arm away and checked it for blood. The hand stayed still in the light, then moved down to grab the bag of food. Deshawn looked on as it was dragged into the shadows. The eyes stayed on him. Gnashing sounds began. A growl, a little girls sigh, wheezing.

Deshawn, realizing his mission was complete, jumped up from the floor and ran up the stairs, back to the safety of the kitchen. Amid the sounds of tearing and chewing, the voice of a little girl prevailed. Suddenly there was quiet and she stepped into

the blurred border between the light and the darkness. Her brown

skin marred by bits of food and dried blood, her white t-shirt also

stained with all forms, totally obscuring the picture of a cartoon

princess on the front. Her shorts were torn and their bright red

color was dimmed by dirt. Around her waist was a chain, the end

of which connected to the back wall. Her eyes followed the sound

of her brother Deshawn's clumsy escape from the basement. Her

hair was a mass of uncontrolled tight curls, dirty and wet in areas.

The centerpiece of all that was the cute brown face of a seven

year old girl. The expression on which was too serious for a girl

her age to have. She stared at the stairway leading upstairs as if

her brother was still here.

A low growl emitted from her cute fat cheeks. "I love you

Deshawn. I'm sorry."

Deshawn, out of breath, scared and his shoulders were

hunched up near his ears. Still facing the door, he backed away

slowly while pulling up his sagging pants that slid off his waist

while running. Deshawn's mind raced with brand new memories

of fear, none of which replaced the old ones, they were just additions to his anxiety.

Walking backwards, he stumbled on the leg of a chair in the kitchen, the loud sound of the chair skidding on the tile startled him and turned him away from the door.

In the midst of his fear based clumsiness, Deshawn caught a glimpse of the case worker standing in the living room hunched over with her hands covering her face. He turned towards the living room and started toward the scene as the case worker let out muffled screams as she stumbled about. He could see in the light what looked like dust particles or smoke floating in the air around the woman. Yolanda calmly walked into the scene, bending over to pick up the case worker's paperwork and suitcase. She carefully placed the papers into the case, closed and locked it. The case worker's writhing slowed, her screaming and moaning stopped.

Yolanda handed the case worker her briefcase, she raised her arm to grab it but her arm flopped down by her side. Her dust stained face was expressionless and her eyes became windows to nothing.

"Now…" Yolanda started, as her index finger made a circle in the air and stopping to pointing at the woman, "…you gon' go back to yo' office, git on yo' computer, and delete everything you got on this family. Do you hear me?" The case worker stood still for a few seconds then slowly nodded her head.

"Y…yes…of course." The caseworker's voice was submissive and soft, "…of course I will." She turned away from Yolanda and started stumbling towards the front door. Her hair was scattered about her head, every step she took shook dust off her head and shoulders.

"Of course I will…yes, I have to go now," she murmured to no one in particular as she turned the knob on the door and stumbled out the house. Yolanda rushed to the door to shut and locked it. She looked over to her son Deshawn, whose mouth was open and on the verge of tears.

"Deshawn, why is you cryin'? C'mere." Yolanda ordered, as she went to him. Wiping tears from his eyes, Yolanda Jenkins' youngest son reluctantly waited for his mother, he wasn't expecting comfort.

"Ayesha grabbed me...and she...ah...." he put his head down and sobbed, it was all too much for him, the police visits, a sick savage sister he didn't know anymore, a careless, unloving mother, another sick family member in the attic, the threats from DCFS to break up the only family he knew and now...

Suddenly, from behind Deshawn appeared the albino twin, Deshawn quickly turned around. The Black twin suddenly appeared at Deshawn's side. He spun back around in shock, he winced and sighed, *these muthafuckas,* he thought to himself.

Yolanda, in a rare show of affection, grabbed Deshawn gently by the back of his head, "Yo' sistah scared you baby?" Deshawn shook his head yes, the tall twins flanking him, bent over slightly as if to console their younger brother.

"Okay, Imma talk to ha..." Yolanda's usual curtness and confidence wavered at the thought of confronting her daughter, Deshawn noticed the momentary lapse in his mother's defenses and just looked up at her in disbelief.

"OKAY?!" Yolanda asked forcefully. Deshawn replied with a simple sheepish "Yea."

"Okay, go back upstairs an' do yo' homework." Yolanda softened her voice after noticing her son's stress. The Black twin extended his hand to touch his younger brother, he managed to caress his afro to which Deshawn looked up at the twin teary eyed, then just walked on.

"But check on yo' granmotha first while you's up there." Deshawn's face crumpled into another round of fear and despair.

Dammit, not her, I jus wanna' do my homework, he lamented quietly. The finality of his mother's command registered with Deshawn as he left the living room and started up the stairs. Yolanda folded her arms and looked down onto the floor as if contemplating the entirety of the scenes that had just played out. The twins waited patiently, unmoving, while their mother stood quietly for a second. She waited to hear Deshawn get far enough up the stairs.

Once she felt comfortable with his distance, she turned to her other sons, "Did'ja' git what I axed?" The two shook their heads simultaneously, then, as if choreographed, both turned to the back of the kitchen, stooped down and retrieved two separate book bags, one black, the other white. Yolanda turned to close the kitchen door behind her, "Ok let's see."

With simultaneous motions, they placed their respective bags on the kitchen table, the Black son reached to unzip his black bag and opened it towards his mother. She leaned over to take a peek inside. It was barely visible in the low light of the kitchen but she was able to see enough of the two rabbits with their bloody heads twisted backwards, "Uh huh, ok, gud."

She then turned to the albino son, "Let's see." He reached across and unzipped his white bag, the mother leaned in for another peek. A human head with the eyes missing and a hand.

"Son, is that ah right hand? I said left." The albino let out a series of low grunts and motioned his head and hands to illustrate an explanation.

"Don't matta', at least he suffed. Gud, bof of y'all. Leave the rabbits, I'll skin them and cook them. Y'all get rid of that other shit." Her orders landed on fertile ears, immediately her twins shuffled their way to do their mother's bidding, their only sounds were slight grunts.

Once they emptied out of the kitchen through the back door, Yolanda Jenkins stood by herself, taking a long breath and reaching up to pull off her wig. Once her head was free, she massaged her small afro, letting the wig float down onto the table. She stared into the open bag at the furry carcasses, the dead eye of the rabbit was open and aimed directly at her, it's glassy surface reflected a distorted image of her being.

Transfixed upon it, with her arms crossed, she took another deep breath and turned her head to look at the door to the basement. She immediately closed and picked up the bag, walked over to the drawer and pulled out the tools needed to skin the animals. The rest of what she needed was exactly where she needed to go.

Carrying all the items, she slowly opened the basement

door and casually started down the stairs for some mother/ daughter quality time.

Deep in the darkness of the basement, even before she made it to the second step, Yolanda could hear her daughter.

"Hello Mother."

A SATURDAY NIGHT IN
BRONZEVILLE

A child suspended in darkness, his breathing shallow and all sound barely audible. He twitched at his own whimper which moved him closer to consciousness. He heard another scant sound along with a flash of color in the bottom of the darkness, then the realization of pain. He could feel the pulsating ache followed by a strange taste in his mouth. He focused on every sensation that returned in a desperate attempt to make sense of something. Every second that passed the blur took more form, the muffled sounds became slightly clearer and the pain vibrated harder. Another whimper stirred him until finally one eye opened. The darkness was pierced by a blur of light as his other eye slowly did the same. He could feel his head was not level and his body was slumped over. An attempt to move resulted in pain radiating through his right jaw and vibrating throughout his face. The more light he saw, the more forms took shape. The more muffled sounds he heard, the more sense they made. There was a beat, a rhythm, then a voice within the rhythm and the beat; all of it was unrecognizable. He slowly sat upright and the ache from his face was now joined by newly emerging pains from his arms, shoulders and back. He drew a shallow breath and exhaled another whimper, followed by a cough that jolted his entire body, making him wince. A sudden, full blast of light blinded him for a few seconds but soon shape and color was restored. He turned his head slightly to his left to survey a room with white walls, windows covered with black curtains and a black sofa directly in front of him. At the far right side of the room, along the wall, was a large blue tarp on the floor. His body squirmed at the annoyance of the unrecognizable music playing. Memories started to take form through the murk of his confusion. He recalled being outside, with his friends, and soon other pieces of the immediate past began to assemble in his mind. He instinctively tried to stand but found he was unable to do so. Upon looking down, he realized he was duct taped to a chair and his feet were also bound. One more dreadful realization hit him as hard as the pain in his face. He was alone and terrified. A child crying alone in a strange, dark place.

Ninety minutes earlier...

FX NOZAKHERE

Thirty-fifth street was bright, loud and rambunctious, which is a usual thing on a Saturday night. The beauty of the dark, blue night sky was at times obscured by the dullness of moving dark overcast clouds which blocked the light of the stars. It was nine-thirty seven pm when the neighborhood regulars gathered on street corners in front of the two liquor stores separated by only a block.

Almost every business on the strip was lit up and open. McDonald's had customers filing in and out, satisfying their early night weed induced munchies. **Harold's Chicken Shack** was crowded with clean yet casually dressed patrons who'd just come from the nearby sports club. The liquor store had the usual characters hanging out in front, slapping hands, laughing, arguing, threatening and cat calling women going in and out of the store. From Michigan to King Drive, the entire street was energized with the souls of Black folks, some tragic, some triumphs.

In the cool, dark night, walking down the street were five tragedies. Young boys who in other neighborhoods would be in their homes, visiting friends, playing video games or being babysat by responsible teenagers. In this neighborhood; however, they were just some of the many regulars out in the streets. Two were eleven, Jeff and Law, one nine, Davey and one six year old, Lil' Zo. All led by a fifteen year old named Patrick. "Trick" was his name in the R.A.I.D.E.R.S., a gang he belonged to which was a splinter group off the aging Blackstone Rangers. They were a mix of former Black Disciples who were left behind when the projects were demolished and replaced by modernized mixed income town and row houses.

For many reasons, the gang wasn't much of a threat to the Bronzeville neighborhood, just a loud and rude nuisance. Tonight Trick aimed to change that. With four new generations of bangers under his wing, he set to make a mark on the streets and introduce him and some of his soldiers to Bronzeville. What better place and time to do that than Thirty-Fifth street on a Saturday night?

His youngest soldier, Lil Zo, didn't want to show his nervousness. Being the smallest one, constantly looked up to the bigger kids but usually he had the loudest voice. His mean face was intimidating to the younger children but the older kids saw through it. Trick wasn't having any of that. For him it was time for Lil Zo, Law, Jeff and Davey to prove their worth. What can they do? How will they act? Who is going to cry? Trick needed these questions answered before he returned the small soldiers to their rightful owners, the gang generals.

The R.A.I.D.E.R.S. were the first gang in a long time to try to form a structure to take advantage of the renegade nature of the streets, this at least was the plan of the generals.

So here they were, walking down the loud street led by a teenager who himself had to prove he was up to the task. There was a lot riding on the success of tonight's activities and it reflected in Lil Zo's face. His usual mean mugging mask wasn't securely in place tonight. Instead there was, at times, a face full of excitement and anticipation, just as with most kids on some new adventure. The other boys held emotionless gazes, only occasionally broken by laughter at the most inappropriate jokes for pre-teens to be hearing.

The boys were dressed in gym shoes, various t-shirts, baggy sagging jeans or shorts. Much of which didn't seem to be appropriate clothing for a cool, sixty-two degree night but none of them gave much thought to the coolness of the air. Instead, their little legs moved with childlike enthusiasm, occasionally bobbing their heads to the latest Rap music blasting from the various passing vehicles.

They weaved in and out of mini crowds, side stepping adults who paid them no mind and never even as much as glance down at children walking the streets at such a late hour. There was never any wonder. Between the hustle and voices echoing throughout Thirty-fifth street, the young boys' conversation just joined the cacophony of noise, hardly noticeable at all.

"Can we get sum MickeyD's?" pleaded Jeff, the eleven year old. "Ay Trick maan, food nigga," he pointed his small arm across the street to the blaring yellow arches.

"Nah man wait." Trick responded.

"C'mon maan, how we gon' do this wit no food? Shit, I'm hungry nigga." Jeffrey said, making his case.

"No! Shut up the hell up lil nigga. We do that shit afta!

Soldiers don't eat til the job is done." Trick's gym shoes pounded the pavement hard in tune to the beat of the house music from the Skatt Brothers blasting from a passing vehicle, his fist forever clenched.

"Fuck you mean?" Davey, the nine year old, asked. His stomach had been growling for a minute so he was in total agreement with Jeff.

"It mean what I say it mean." Trick shot back. Trick found immediate agreement from Law.

"We solja's right? You a solja is you?" He spit this question at Jeff.

"Yeah!" Jeff reassured himself as much as he reassured Law and Trick. It was a shaky confidence Lil Zo fed off for himself.

"They said we could keep what we snatch, I can get y'all sumthn' wit that…" Trick instructed. "But we gots ta get it first, a'ight?" There was no response. "Iz dat alright wit y'all?!" Trick stared down at the younger ones to elicit a response to his leadership.

Law, "A'ight."

Jeff, "A'ight"

Lil Zo, "Yeah."

Davey, "A'ight Trick."

"Now who holdin?" Trick asked as he continued his rhythmic step down Thirty-fifth street. The four youngsters walked in silence, some looking down, others looking around at the others. So he repeated the question,"who holdin?"

Still silence. Lil Zo looked around at the other boys, his throat growing tight and his heart thumping in his tiny chest. He waited for the other boys to offer themselves up but no one stepped up. *I can do that!* he thought, *but should I?* He asked himself, searching for courage within.

As he walked for what seemed like hours in his little mind, he played the visual in his head of holding a gun, aiming it then pulling the trigger. He saw himself jump at the sound, the flash of light and the smoke coming from the barrel. He had visions of

Davey, Jeff, Law yelling and cheering his name with Trick standing in awe. Trick, he was the one that mattered the most; he was the one that would tell the tale to the generals of Lil Zo putting in that work. That would also be the start of him getting back at Trick for what he'd done weeks ago at Trick's house.

Lil Zo's fear of Trick was only surpassed by his hatred for him, which was complicated by his need to gain favor with Trick in order to look good in the eyes of the generals. That would give him the leverage he needed to extract pay back.

"I'll do it." Trick looked back in the direction of the boys, trying to determine which one had volunteered.

"Who?" he asked.

"I'll do it! Gimme it," nine year old Davey demanded. Lil Zo's head jerked in Davey's direction; he was too young *not* to show emotion on his face. It was a betrayal Davey knew nothing about but Lil Zo needed that gun.

"Nah' I…I'll do it." Zo finally got the courage to speak up. Desperation can be a powerful thing.

"You too small nigga! The gun bigga than you!" Davey's remark brought snickering from the others. Their laughter stung Lil Zo in his chest.

"I can shoot it betta' than you bitch!" He fired back to protect his undeveloped ego. He looked to Trick who had already turned his head away from them, something ahead had caught his attention.

The five boys walked north on deserted Federal street then east down towards the action. They crossed streets against the light, peering into every store window, looking into cars as they slowly drove pass them. Not one step was idle nor were their minds.

Trick led them past Indiana Avenue and a women yelling, "You ain't gettin' in this pussy no mo!" Pass Giles Avenue with a man shouting, "You want mild or hot on yo wings?!" Pass King Drive where an anonymous voice yelled "I love ya man!"

Trick's attention was focused on the silhouette of a couple walking further down 35th Street. He'd spotted them a few blocks back, keeping track of them as he concentrated on keeping the young soldiers in line. He was trying to gauge how far east they were walking and where they could potentially end up. Trick was looking for an opportunity.

A Walk After the Show

A young couple strolled down the block laughing, talking, yelling then laughing again. They were two of the remaining people leaving the festivities at Washington Park and walking north on King Drive. When every other small group stopped at various houses, bus shelters or turned down side streets, Jahn and Araminta continued their forward route.

"...Oh and Jahn, the dancers! The girl doing ballet?!" Araminta's eyes grew wide reminiscing "They were beautiful..."

Jahn interrupted "Graceful."

"Graceful!" Araminta's voice lifted "That broad...I think she may have been taught by one of my teachers, she was just that good!"

"They played off one another well but I was expecting her cavalier to go on the pole with her." Jahn added.

"Oh, now that would have been freaking awesome!" Araminta replied laughing. The couple slowly walked in and out of the shadows cast by the trees obscuring the street lights.

Once within the light, Araminta's locs swayed back and forth over her honey brown face, in time with every accent laced word she spoke. Her pitch black locs laid midway down her gray, waist length coat.

Jahn's silhouette in the darkness showed a squared shouldered man topped with a full mane of hair. Once out of the shadows, the light revealed a black dress coat covering broad shoulders and a golden brown complexion contrasted by a almost blue-black goatee. His mane was a full head of thick black locs that reached his shoulders.

"But I have to admit Jahn, I'm not very pleased with the use of the animals, but that's not nearly as bad as what was done to those two boys with Ringling Brothers." Her voice turned ominous.

"The Brothers Muse, terrible what they did to them! I wanted to help them so bad..." Jahn's face changed. "...But no matter how much solicitude I had for those poor boys…" Before

he could finish, Araminta looked up to face him, her eyes and

words matching his melancholy.

"There was not much we could do at that time, we had our

own battles. I too wanted to free the young men myself, harshly I

might add."

Jahn looked down at the shorter Araminta, a subtle smile

emerging in response to her solace.

"One of many regrets." He replied simply.

"But that's ok, now we have the Cirque du Universoul and

while I don't like the use of the animals, I prefer Universoul over

those oppressive Barnum and Bailey bastards!" She finished her

tirade, ending with a perfect pirouette. Her antics pulled a hearty

laugh out of Jahn who held her hand above her head as she spun

again.

In the cool, dark night, the young couple blended well

with the natives of Bronzeville…

"Yo Trick, give it to me." Davey insisted. Lil Zo sped up

to get Trick's attention.

DuSable City

They finally stopped at Tricks' non-verbal command and set up a huddle in a darkened part of the street several feet from the corner next to White Castle. The corner was loosely populated with people waiting at a bus stop while others were just hanging out. Smelling the aroma of the famous White Castle sliders had Lil Zo's stomach growling. He knew the other boys were hungry as well. They rarely had money for food but the prospect of eating after taking care of business was incentive enough to get things done as fast as possible. The sooner they did this, the sooner they could eat some burgers. It was a reward with the biggest prize going to the one that could show they could handle business as well.

Lil Zo was surprised the two eleven-year old boys hadn't volunteered for the work, only his six-year old self and the nine-year old Davey who was about to steal his opportunity.

"A'ight, huddle up closer." Trick took center post in the darkened area of the sidewalk away from the crowd near the parking lot.

"Who holdin'?" he asked again, having not taken the two

younger boys seriously. Davey immediately interjected, "I got it, give it to me."

Lil Zo responded forcefully, "Nah man, I got it Trick."

Trick tucked his hand into his sweater pocket, it had been weighing him down on this long walk. He looked at Davey, nine years old and a little too eager to want to change his life forever. He thought about the stories the generals told him about their first time, the youngest of them had been nine, the same as Davey. Trick peered over to Lil Zo and analyzed his small body, *can he even hold the damn thing* he reasoned within himself.

He kept his eyes on Lil Zo a little longer, contemplating the ramifications of choosing the first grader. His hesitations gave way to the idea that *he* could beat the generals' youngest age by "busting his cherry" as they called it. How would he look in the eyes of the men running this whole organization if he oversaw a young shooter in the making at just six years old? Such an achievement would net him a prominent spot in the organization.

He looked down the street to see how far the couple

walked. He winced his eyes to focus on them engaged in an intimate hug near the corner of Rhodes, waiting for cars to pass. *Good*, he thought, they weren't too far.

Trick turned to Lil Zo, "Zo, if I give you this, can you handle it?"

"Nah he cain't! Trick..." Davey protested.

Lil Zo's heart raced with excitement, "Yeah, I held a gun befo'." He lied. He would say whatever he had to for his opportunity.

"No, he didn't! Dis lil ho ain't never hold shit! The only gun he ever held was a video game gun!" Davey shouted.

"Yo! Chill yo voice little nigga!" Law interjected. "Aye, if you don't think Zo can do it, I got it."

Trick looked at Lil Zo, he knew the little boy better than the others. His mind flashed back to the time at his house. The generals were using it to stash contraband after a job. Lil Zo was in the living room playing video games with Davey and two other children. Zo was the only one who took a visible interest in what was going on. His persistence at peeking in on grown up business annoyed the generals but it intrigued Trick. It intrigued him enough to take advantage of the naive curiosity of the little boy later that night by indulging his own twisted curiosity. It was an indulgence that had elicited vengeful thoughts in Lil Zo once he realized his victim hood.

Trick made up his mind. "Here Zo." Pulling a black nine millimeter from his sweater pocket, he carefully placed it in the small, eager hands of Zo.

"Maaaan…" Davey whined.

"Man shut yo' little ass up! If this go right, you gon' get yo chance. Maybe even lata tonight." Trick's words were meant to put Davey at ease and mentally prepare him for what was about to happen.

"Put it down yo' pants." Trick ordered, looking back to where the couple was, they had already started walking further east. He immediately helped stuff the pistol down Lil Zo's small pants, never taking caution with the trigger. He tucked it into the waist of the little boy's jeans causing an uncomfortable look on his face at having Trick put his hands on him. It brought back particular memories but he had no time for revulsion, he had been chosen and he didn't want to disappoint. For in the mind of this six-year old was a long term plan, a plan that started with tonight's showcase...

Hand in hand, the couple moved slowly in step with one another toward the corner, instinctively stopping at the curb.

"All we have gone through, all we have seen, and, for example, gander at the street behind us. It...it feels like, like nothing has ever happened." She gripped Jahn's hand with every point she made. Jahn inhaled sharply, paused, then sighed, shaking his head.

"Far be it for me to extol the virtues of hope." Araminta looked up at him, hanging on his every word.

"I want to hope that there could be a redemption for our people. But nowadays..." His words ended as if the change in the traffic light interrupted him. Some lights turned green while other turned red, the colors reflected off the streets, the vehicles and the faces of the couple stepping off the curb. Their coats blended together as they fluttered in an occasional wind gust.

"Jahn, why do you feel that way about hope?" Araminta interrupted.

"Mostly I feel what you feel Minta, your disappointment." Jahn revealed. "And just as I feel your disappointment, I feel...I feel as if there's something else..."

Araminta's brow furrowed as she turned her head for a direct look into his eyes. She waited for the rest of his thought.

Jahn continued after a short pause "...Something else beyond just our disappointments, like there's more to come."

Araminta continued to stare into Jahn's eyes, and for once tonight, she had nothing to say. Since they'd left Washington Park, her face had gone from wide eyes and smiles to expressions of regret and anger.

"Well, as if we did not have a crock of other things to think about." Araminta replied finally, as she tilted her head on Jahn's shoulder.

The couple continued past the medium momentarily

looking up at the war monument standing prominently over King Drive. Upon reaching the east side of the street, with no words and no instigation, Araminta stood on her tip toes and kissed Jahn on his cheek.

...

"A'ight c'mon..." Trick started walking fast, following after the couple, "...see them down there?" The boys, while trying to keep up, strained their eyes to view what Trick pointed out. Three of them responded with an affirmative "Yeah."

"C'mon, that's what we hittin'! If they turn down Lake Park, we got they ass!" Trick's voice lifted with excitement, he looked over at Lil Zo struggle to maintaining a cool composure while working hard to keep the nine millimeter secure.

"Aye lil nigga, don't fuck this up, you ain't a baby no mo afta this."

Lil Zo figured out a way to walk while simultaneously hiding the piece and keeping it secure so he wouldn't drop it. This was it, his chance to make his mark and set things right. The video in his mind of how everything was to play out repeated then

paused. Out of his peripheral, he caught Davey glance a menacing

look at him and then shake his head. *Fuck him,* he thought, *I'm

ready for this! He'll see, the generals will see and most of all,

Trick will see. In fact, he'll do more than see.*

Just as Trick had hoped, the couple made a southern turn

down Lake Park, a dark, deserted street. He gave out the last

directives before the boys went their separate ways to play out

their positions and change their lives forever. A darker shadow

moved through the dark shadows, the only sound made was the

breeze rushing through trees and the subtle talk of a man and

woman. The vacant lots, crowded alleys and darkened row houses

characterized this Lake Park section of Bronzeville, a stark

contrast to the cleanliness and historical markers of King Drive.

The few street lamps cast a dim dirty light onto the

concrete. The light was dissected by shadows from tree branches

and overhead wire. The street was empty for as far as the couple

could see. The man was dressed in a long black coat, his dread-

locs hanging down his back. The woman were a long dark-brown coat topped with a light-brown fur collar and lapel. They walked slowly, occasionally bumping into each other and holding hands. Their simultaneous laughter set a tone of lightheartedness that separated them from the street and carved their way through whatever wretchedness the south side of Chicago had to offer. But, on the empty street, they both noticed a little boy walking towards them.

Lil Zo power walked toward the couple, fumbling with the waistband of his pants to get the gun out and ready. Whatever smooth actions he'd envisioned were immediately erased by reality, fear and inexperience.

Finally, grabbing a hold of the handle, the gun emerged pointed and ready. "RUN YO' SHIT BITCH!" He managed to have some conviction in his voice as he stopped and stood his ground, looking up at the couple in front of him.

The couple stopped walking, they stopped holding hands and laughing. They both just peered down at the assailant in their path.

"The fuck?" The woman uttered in disbelief. The man tilted his head to the left, a lone loc swayed forward.

"Whoa…wait little man! You might want to chill with that." He never moved, never stuck his hand out and never stepped in front of the woman with him.

"Shut tha fuck up! Gimmee yo wa…wallet, yo' purse bitch…run dat shit now!" Lil Zo put as much bass into his little voice as he could muster but it was only the high-pitched, congested voice of a child. His was demanding but it didn't invoke terror or movement from the would-be victims.

The woman bent over slightly, as if to get a closer look at Lil Zo and said, "It's a little boy with a gun as big as he is…" A shadow rushed behind her and an elbow smashed into the back of her head. With a grunt, the woman went down, head first down into the pavement. The man barely moved, instead he just casually turned his head in the direction of the assailant. It was Trick followed by Davey.

"He said run yo' shit nigga! We ain't fuckin' playin'

witcho' muh-fuckin ass!" Trick's voice had the bass needed to demand what he wanted. His past experience gave him just enough confidence to ensure a successful robbery...at least in his mind.

"All y'all need to just relax, I'll get my..." Trick interrupted the man with a gun pushed in his face. Lil Zo still stood petrified, holding his gun at the man, "I got it!" he yelled. Behind him, Jeff and Law walked up, surrounding the man and the fallen woman.

Upon seeing two more child-robbers, the man finally raised his hands but only slightly. He let out a sigh.

"You don't have to do this. Y'all can go about your business, leave us alone and we won't even call the police." He looked down at the woman who was rubbing the back of her head. "Because when she gets back up..." Trick pressed his finger against the trigger, pushing the gun closer to the man's head.

"I don't give a fuck about that bitch! I'll blow yo fuckin' brains out nigga..."

"Trick, I got it man!" Lil Zo yelled.

Trick turned to Zo, "...get that bitches shit!"

There was a swift shuffle of feet, the gun was knocked out of Trick's hand before he could get the next curse word out. The man landed a backhand to his face, sending him flying several feet away. The woman jumped up suddenly and looked directly at Lil Zo between the hair covering her face. Lil Zo kept the gun pointed, his eyes widened and his mouth dropped, he tried to yell out a command but he was cut off by Law and Jeff running towards the woman in attack mode. She quickly turned her focus on the two eleven-year old boys.

With barely a sound, she jumped onto Jeff and quickly overwhelmed him until there was an explosion of blood from his body as her gnawed at his neck. His scream was loud but it quickly ended. Law slid to stop his momentum towards Jeff's nearly decapitated body. He whimpered pathetically at the sight of the woman standing, her coat stained with Jeff's blood as she continued to gnaw at his shredded neck.

DuSable City

The man had already grabbed Davey by the back of his neck, squeezing hard. He spun Davey's little body around then lifted him to his mouth, ripping off pieces of his face. Blood pooled from the gaping hole in Davey's former face as the man latched on and began to drink.

Trick began stirring on the ground several feet away from the gruesome scene. Lil Zo looked at him with the hope he would get up and stop what was happening. He was still holding the gun, pointing it at the scene in front of him. The sounds of brief screaming followed by quiet then flesh tearing and slurping, violated his young ears. He was frozen. His only movement was his little finger trying to squeeze the trigger. The woman caught sight of his movement. Flashing a bloody smile, she rushed Lil Zo. His eyes never caught a full view of her movement, she was in one spot then he suddenly felt an explosion of pain against his jaw, immediately sending him to the concrete and the gun flew from his hand. It was a full impact punch that left a bloody fist print on the right side of his face and had him spread-eagle on the concrete. He was out.

He didn't have time to cry.

He never even screamed. But there was no respite from the scene by being unconscious.

Seconds later, his eyes opened again. He could feel the pain on the right side of his face but he was in too much shock to cry. He was able to lift his head just enough to see the aftermath.

The woman was clawing at Law's back, his clothes were bloody and tattered, she kept ripping and tearing until his vertebrae could be seen between ribbons of red flesh.

The man walked over to Trick, who was crawling towards Lil Zo.

"Z...zo...." he uttered. The man flung his head around and his locs flew gracefully behind him. He grabbed Trick by the back of his neck, lifted him until his feet dangled, carried him to the nearest parked car and drove his face into the driver's side window; the glass cracked. Not satisfied with that, the man rammed Trick's face into the window four more times, until the window was a blue spider web of cracks accentuated by blood and flesh from the face of the teenager.

Lil Zo tasted stomach bile racing into his mouth, he turned over and threw up his inner contents onto the concrete. The vomit mixed with the blood flowing from Law, Jeff and Davey. There was no way to tell what blood belonged to whom. The concrete around the scene was a dark maroon mixed with bottles, used condoms and hamburger wrappers, the last thing Lil Zo saw before passing out again.

As he slowly faded into unconsciousness, he could hear voices but none of them were familiar.

"Ugh, what a mess."

"This is mostly you, I got this one here oh and that one."

"Can't believe no one saw that."

"What happened to him?"

"Oh…I did that."

"You punched a baby? You're a monster."

She snickered.

Then there was nothing.

Lil Zo awakened to drool and blood slipping off his face, his vision blurred and his hearing irritated by the sudden blast of singing. Before he could assess where he was he heard a voice behind the music, it was coming from another room behind him. Following right behind the voice was a loud thump. Just then a figure came into his vision from the left, his eyes focused enough to see it was a man moving about the living room. Jahn strutted in to the music, popping his fingers with his eyes closed while shaking his head to the beat. He wore black slacks and a white button up shirt that had red stains on the front. He turned his head to Lil Zo and shot him a look between his moves then returned to focusing on the beat. His locs swung with the music. Lil Zo stared in dual fear and confusion, a combination that did not abate when the man started lip syncing the words of the song while still dancing. If there was no duct tape over Lil Zo's mouth, it would have been wide open. His eyes were already transfixed on the dancer in front of him.

DuSable City

As the music started a soulful build up, the man was suddenly joined by a woman. Araminta slowly walked in step with the music in a blood stained spaghetti strap tank top and Kente Cloth skirt that adorned her slender body, her locs swayed slightly with her movements.

The music slowed as Araminta turned to stare into the eyes of this eight year old boy. Her dancing ceased as she walked slowly towards Lil Zo, whose fear began to rise with every note from the music. His mind was a complete mesh of confusion, his eyes were watered and dilated above the gray duct tape. His shoulders hunched and his head leaned back as Araminta came closer to him. The hope that the man and woman in front of him were not the same man and woman who hurt him outside was fleeting. Araminta flashed a slight smile at Lil Zo then pointed to his left. Zo turned his head to where she pointed and suddenly realized that Trick was behind him, duct taped to a chair. The teens' head was hanging over in an unnatural position with areas of his neck missing. Flimsy flaps of skin were hanging off his face along with his eye dangling inches from its' socket. The boy jumped and screamed under the duct tape. He tried to scoot the chair away from what was left of Trick but froze when the woman re-captured his attention.

With a very unsettling smile, she knelt in front of Zo, pointing to his right. His head shook and moved slowly, his eyes closed tight. He finally opened them to see Jahn holding one end of a large blue tarp that was on the floor. Once certain he had Zo's undivided attention, Jahn dramatically yanked the cover from the floor, revealing what was underneath. A pile of young boys' bloodied and dismembered bodies flooded his vision as terror flooded his young mind.. All Zo's questions were immediately answered. His chest and abdomen started heaving frantically as tears streamed down his face, flowing over the gray duct tape. He managed another muffled scream under the gag, hoping to reach the ears of anyone outside of wherever he was. He rocked the chair back and forth as his vision became blurry from the flood of tears.

Lil Zo turned his head from the grotesque sight right into the face of Araminta, who now had a red glow in her eyes and a large smile revealing four sharp fangs just underneath her lips. Lil

Zo screamed again so hard, he almost choked under the tape.

Araminta stared at the boys' reaction until her smile disappeared.

"Oh no, no, no…do not cry baby boy," she said in a

soft voice. She move slightly closer to Lil Zo. He had no choice

but to peer into her face, his eyes darting frantically as he recoiled

at the sight of her bright red eyes.

"You were not such a little baby when you pointed your

gun at us, now were you? Now there are tears… now you want to

cry!" Araminta took an account of the evening. She pointed to

Trick

"You know when that one hit me, it actually fucking hurt."

Jahn, standing behind Araminta, slowly looked up to reveal the

same red glow emanating from his eyes. Four fangs revealed

themselves as he offered his polite answer in a smooth voice.

"In more than one way."

"Yes indeed, it did. So now you do not get to cry! So shut

your damn mouth!" Araminta exclaimed. "If you indeed had any balls descending from your prepubescent body, you would have shot me dead!"

"And all this on a school night..." Jahn smirked and shook his head. "...Anyway, we need to figure out what we're going to do with these bodies." The angry look on her face faded into contemplation as she thought about what to do with Lil Zo.

"And him." Jahn added. Araminta sighed, stretched the muscles of her slender body and turned to Jahn.

"And who is him?" She asked, with a bored expression.

"Little Lorenzo Jackson. Eight years old, lives on thirty something and Calumet. You are a Raiders' Disciple or something..." Jahn rolled his eyes and turned to Araminta, "...that's a gang my dear..." The woman feigned being impressed while the man continued.

"Your mother is...who knows where? Your father? Selling drugs somewhere? A brother that was killed, a grandmother at home probably worried for you and despite all of that, you are a still straight A student at Reaves' Elementary? Shame." The man looked at Lorenzo shaking his head.

With tears drying on his face, Lorenzo gave up his struggle against the binding tightness of the duct tape, his body starting to slump as he was out of breath.

"Oh yeah, your positive role model here told us everything. It was easy getting information and secrets out of him when we peeled off chunks of his body and dangled them in his ruined face. Addresses, family members and..." Jahn's voice trailed off into Araminta's voice.

"...Confessions. He touched you, did he not? Well, you need not worry about that anymore...you are welcome." Araminta interjected. Lorenzo stopped fidgeting, his visions of shooting Trick dashing violently against the force of the two things before him. He let out another whimper.

"Let's hear what he wants to say dear," the man said softly. The woman bent over and extended her hands to slowly and gently pull the tear drenched duct tape from Lorenzo's mouth. His eyes shot back and forth between Patrick's body and the woman.

Once his mouth was freed, Lorenzo took a breath and exhaled words.

"Let me go...p...please. I...I wanna go ho..."

"Home?!" Araminta interrupted, "Now you want to go home? And what home are you talking about?! What home are you going to boy?! Where is your mother? Why isn't your father here to protect you? You want your granny? An' who are you going to tell about what you have seen here tonight?"

Jahn now stooped to Lorenzo's eye level. "We know what he did to you and you see what we did to him. Now what would you have done? Maybe shoot him? Your little body wouldn't have handled the recoil of that gun. You would have just injured him and hurt yourself, maybe even missed him and hit someone else. Look what we've done...we gave you the revenge you wanted. In your hardened little heart, your revenge is not being torn apart like him, but you still might end up like that...which brings us to this conundrum. What are we going to do with you kid?" He pointed his index finger gently into Lorenzo's chest.

"Please don't kill me!" Lorenzo pleaded.

"I am full from draining the others, but I could feast some more." Araminta's bright red eyes blinked as she turned to Jahn.

"I'm sorry! I'm sorry!" Lorenzo's voice cracked amid more tears.

The man sighed, "I don't know…is it even worth it? Is he even worth it?"

With tears in his eyes, a face in pain, friends dead, no hope and no help…with all his frustration, all his pain and with all his breath, Lorenzo's whole face morphed into something angry and unrecognizable.

"FF….FUCK YOU! FUCK YOU!! I HATE YOU!!! FUCK YOU!!! I'LL KILL YOU!!! I'LL… KILL …YOU!!!" He turned to Trick's body, "I'LL KILL YOU!!!!!"

Jahn's red eyes grew wide at the explosion and the transformation. He then closed them, lowered and shook his head at the same time, all while smirking. He slowly brought his head back up and exclaimed.

"AH! There it is! I knew it was there Minta! That's what pointed that gun at us tonight! Not the little boy!" The woman's impassive expression never changed. She stood with her arms folded, unaffected and unmoved, while staring at a child losing his mind.

"The blood tastes so much better when they're all hot and excited like that." She said in a calm low voice, her fangs were prominent between her open lips. She moved her tongue over their pointed tips.

"That it does. That....it....does." Jahn responded.

The couple stared calmly at Lorenzo Jackson as he rocked his body against the binds and screamed with a face soiled with dried tears, blood and duct tape fibers. They had started their evening with laughter and fond memories. It had now transformed into something else, as had they. For the first time in a long time, little Lorenzo Jackson felt eight years old. He cried and raged until his voice and his tiny body gave out.

Three fifteen in the morning.

Several large laundry bags crowded a backseat as an arm reached in and pulled one out. The only light offered within the dark was from the full moon. Dim street lamps from the alley on the other side of a wall and the orange side lights from a sedan provided some ghostly shadows to accompany the supernatural scene. Jahn had hold of one of the bags and flung it into a hollowed out section of dirt. The other host of this macabre night sat in a lawn chair, legs crossed and cradling a cup of tea. A shovel was stabbed into the ground beside her. He grunted as he reached into the backseat to pull out another laundry bag. Before tossing it into the crater, he turned to Araminta.

"Are you sure about what we will do with that boy?" He voice held the slightest bit of uncertainty. Araminta looked up from her tea with a raised eyebrow. There was no uncertainty at all in her response.

"Very sure." She responded, while her crossed leg bounced up and down on the other.

"Very well then." There was silence.

After a time, Jahn slid the last bag from the backseat. Just as he was about to fling it, he paused. After a few seconds, he picked up the bag with both hands, walked over to the hole and gently released it. The bag landed softly on top of the pile of unfortunates. Araminta looked up from sipping her tea.

"Jahn, getting back to what we were talking about earlier before we were rudely interrupted; why do you feel like there's no hope?" Jahn took a few seconds and surveyed the scene around them.

"Really Araminta?"

"You said you felt something else, what did you feel?" She ignored the sarcasm in his tone. Now staring at the hollow before them, Jahn took a breath and slightly shook his head.

"Well, for one, of all the things we've done, there's no coming back from this..."

"What do you m..." Just as she was about to continue, they both noticed headlights in the distance. The lights switched off and the street lights partially revealed a SUV winding through the pathway of the cemetery. The couple stared at what might be discovery. Jahn stepped to the driver's side of the vehicle and reached in to turn off the side lights. They readied themselves to keep their undertakings from being discovered. However, the SUV never stopped or even slowed. Instead, it made a left turn and proceeded towards the other side of the grounds. The couple breathed a dual sigh of relief but Araminta had to be sure.

"Finish here and I will go make sure the bloke keeps his business." Jahn quickly started the long process of the cover up while Araminta tiptoed through the uneven dirt and quietly made her way to the section where the SUV was heading. Despite the darkness, she made her way through as if her path was well lit… never stumbling, never stopping.

After some time, she could see the outline of the SUV in the faint light of street lamps that barely reached that side of the grounds. She came upon the scene just as the driver turned on the headlights and exited the vehicle. *Amateur,* she thought to herself, as she moved behind a tree and waited. Either she was going to witness something or she was going to *do* something far worse.

Araminta waited patiently as the stranger reached into the back of the vehicle, pulled out a shovel, placed it on the ground and disappeared inside the vehicle. After a few seconds of pulling and grunting, the man appeared again with what looked to be a white sheet shaped like a torso. He struggled to move the wrapped stiffness from the vehicle to the ground. Once he'd gently placed it, Dr. David Wesley turned to the shovel, picked it up and began the painstaking work of digging a fresh grave.

FROM A COLD DARK PLACE

Inside a still, stale and silent room, a wall is covered by large storage units of hollowed steel. Behind each drawer there contains a story. It is eleven fifty eight on the clock in this cold, motionless room.

The full moon shoots pale light through the windows, many of which are covered by dingy beige blinds. The moonlight is brighter than even the one florescent light still working and hanging dangerously from the ceiling. The red and white floor tiles have aged with time from the steps of many who have scoured this space. In the middle of the floor is a drain, the floor tilts ever so slightly towards it.

Spaced about the room are three gurneys; two are empty save for a series of crusted red stains at the end of one of them; the shine of the steel is obscured by the shadow of the wall which blocks out the night light. The other is positioned on the opposite side of the room, with a long translucent tube placed in the middle with the end hanging over the edge, quietly dripping some substance onto the floor. At the opposite end, where the other tables stood, the floor is stained from years of chemical smeared residue pointing like warped arrows towards the drain.

Attached to the remaining walls are four white porcelain sinks, above them are glass cabinets containing an array of powerful chemicals. Moon light illuminates twelve giant squares that compose the side wall. All are stainless steel, complete with shiny handles on the side of each square, and appear to be massive doors made into the wall.

Piercing the silence was a loud thump, emanating from the wall of squares, followed seconds later by a low rustling sound. A steel door flew open from the wall. It clanged as it hit the frame of the cabinet and started to slowly swing back. A scraping sound came from within and out rolled a steel tray; on top of the tray was a long, black bag. A large zipper extends the entire length of the right side of the body bag.

Minutes pass.

Then from the top of the bag comes a small clicking

sound as the zipper slowly begins to move. It slides from the top of the bag, moved by invisible fingers, down the entire length of the right side following the zipper track. As if there was a wind blowing within the room, the ends of the unzipped bag bend upward and away, revealing what was hidden within, a human, nude body. Its skin brown yet pale, wrinkled, and fallen to the sides. Its eyes are closed and sunken into the orbital sockets. The fingers and toes are decorated with paint to distract or cover up the calluses and dryness of the hands, heels and soles. Upon its' head is hair in an afro-style but frayed, with a mix of black and gray.

Hours passed as this naked body lay as if waiting for something to happen. Something did. The ceiling light flickers on, then off. The dingy beige blinds gently flutter outward once from a closed window. The lights flickered back on. The body shook gently, a movement that was almost imperceptible.

"AAAAAAHHHHHHHH!"

The mouth widened and exhaled as the eyes shot open. The jaw made clicking sounds as the mandible shifted left to right while opening. The chest, with its' sunken breasts rose, then the abdomen rose with it and they lowered together. The body took in air and wheezed it out upon exhalation. It continued wheezing breaths for a minute while the eyes first stared into the ceiling then slowly rolled around in the skull as if in search of something.

Bones started crackling even before there was any movement. The shoulders, elbows, wrists, hips, knees and ankles shook subtly, each time causing more dense crackling and popping noises. The entirety of the naked body started to stretch and grow of its' own accord, toes began wiggling, fingers twitching.

Finally, movement in the neck was attempted. It stretched upward with the rest of the body while the paleness of the brown skin began to recede, flush red and then brown as blood rushed into the tissues, activating its melanin. The light flickered on and off, on, then off again, then back on.

As light and darkness dance this macabre dance, the body slowly began to sit up. The lights flickered out and this time they stayed off. The steel tray buckled under the pressure of weight as the body shifted from side to side. The movement in the darkness was accompanied by wheezing and steel popping until there was silence, then the slight sound of bare feet slapping red and white tiles.

"Aaa...aaa...aahhhhh...." a stuttered sigh emanated from the dark half of the room as the body sat on the edge of the table. After a pause, it lifted itself onto the cold, dirty floor. The moonlight was eclipsed by a figure slowly stalking towards the light. A full silhouette takes form against the backdrop of light; it is the silhouette of a five foot six rounded and hunched female.

Bones continue to creak as the figure stretched upright with both arms almost abnormally extended. Every movement is segmented by the popping of bones and joints. The rounded shape transfigures slowly with the sound of bones moving and sliding. Its' skin stretches and twists to accommodate the evolving shape. The body tilts from one side to the other until finally standing straight erect. After it transformed from the rounded shape to a more hourglass figure, all movement stops.

This human thing surveys its environment, focusing on

the table in the semi-darkness. It stumbles over a few steps as it heads for the table. A hand stretches out to pick up a large leather bag left open while the other hand reaches inside to shuffle through the internal objects. Keys, a wallet, identification and some clothes are stuffed deep inside.

Each movement makes it easier for the body to clothe itself but the process is slow. Using unused fingers to button up a white shirt, faded blue jeans, lace up white gym shoes and add a jewel encrusted blue cap with a large bill took ample time and effort. However, these movements helped the bones and joints become more fluid as the body prepares to depart this dark, dismal place.

It was one minute after three am, the door leading out of the room was locked as usual. The outside hallway bulbs were out, with the only illumination coming from an "exit" sign as it emitted a dirty green and yellow mix of light. It barely made the outline of the door perceptible. The yellow brick walls faded into darkness down the hall away from the door and along with them, scuff marks and old tape. There was no sound except a dull hum from the heating system keeping the building warm on an unseasonably cold November night in Chicago.

The low sound of movement comes from within the room. There is the unmistakable sound of feet sliding across a tiled floor; it is a sound that should *not* be coming from this particular locked room at three in the morning. There is a thump on the door then more shuffling. The doorknob begins to slowly turn but handle hits the lock, stops and snaps back into position. The knob twists again slowly, it hits the lock yet continues to turn past the locking mechanism, creating a new sound from within. The sound of metal grinding against metal proceeds the door suddenly opening.

In the doorway stands the newly animated figure. The door, on a spring, would normally close by itself but it stayed open with nothing supporting it. Something had suspended it, something unseen. The dull yellow and green light from the exit sign flickers out, plunging the hallway into total darkness.

The shuffling of feet begins as the woman leaves the doorway to cross the hallway. It was a slow, limping movement to the elevators, where a dark appendage reaches out to slowly push the button until the light illuminates a wrinkled hand. That hand then fell back to the side of the dark figure.

With hardly anyone in this part of the building at this hour, the elevator came quickly, with doors flying open and immediately, perfectly rectangular light broke through the darkness of the basement. A long wheezing breath emanated from the figure as it plodded towards the light, entering the elevator. A clear outline against the light reveals the slightly hunched body of a woman, barely carrying a purse, with disheveled clothes and hair. Once inside the elevator car, the doors immediately slide to a close.

One floor up, the voices of a few nurses behind the emergency room doors can barely be heard. Outside the E.R. is the lobby with opening doorways into the cafeteria, the emergency room, a stairwell and sections of row chairs behind a half wall divider. Within this area sat five people, all waiting to either be seen or for someone to come out.

Two men are huddled together in the corner against the wall, one laying his sleeping head upon the shoulder of the wide awake other, while he stares out the window of the waiting area into nothing. A woman, whose head is buried in her folded arms resting on her lap, sits across from the two men. She is holding a white napkin with small spots of blood. Her rocking back and forth is witnessed by another young male across from her and to the right. His legs are sprawled out and his dirty gym shoes blocking the small aisle. A woman, dressed in a Chicago Bulls starter jacket, steps over the young man's legs to get to her seat in the waiting area. Once seated, she crosses her legs and rests her head on her hand.

A security guard sits at a wooden podium, at times watching over the waiting area, contemplating telling the young man to move his feet from the aisle. Other times, he too is staring out the window. The most movement comes from him, a bored older man with an afro and clothed in a dark blue security uniform. He desires a quick end to his long shift. In order to seemingly speed up the time, he rises from the seat at the podium and walks off into the darkened area of the main lobby. As soon as he disappears to start his patrol, the elevator door slides open, a "ding" sound accompanies its arrival.

Not one head turns to look at what is to come out of the elevator.

The people in the waiting area stay still. The workers in the emergency room entrance; nurses, janitors, doctors, shuffle about tending to their business. They carry mops, files, needles and packages as they performed their duties, never noticing the elevator occupant about to emerge through those sliding doors.

After a long pause, the elevator doors start to roll close but stop in mid motion and reverse to open. The foot shuffling starts and the figure emerges from the elevator, hunched over and wheezing.

Not one head turns to look at what has come out of the elevator.

The figure stops, the vertebrae straining, as the neck twists to turn the head slowly, to survey the area. Eyes that were sunken minutes before view the area as they begin to take shape within the expanding skull. Beyond the waiting area there is a large window, the same window the lobby inhabitant is presently staring out of. The figures' foot moves forward, taking a step across the long, cold lobby floor. All sound is muffled by the waiting room television. Barely audible wheezing grows louder with each labored step the figure takes. It angles its body towards the front lobby door around the corner, the same area where the security guard has just started his patrol.

Not one head in the lobby turns to look at what is slowly moving across the area.

With another wheeze, the bent over husk lumbers towards the main entrance. Past the emergency room automatic doors, no one inside saw it. Past the closed cafeteria doors, where no one heard it. Past the waiting area where it rambles slowly, brushing up against the dividing wall. Still, no one raises their head in its direction. Finally, it disappears into the unlit main lobby, turning its' body while skidding the wall.

Sliding its way to the main doors, it reaches out to push them open only to be stopped by locks. With what seems like an effortless movement, the horizontal door handle presses in, the clicking sound of a latch releases and the door somehow swings opens. Moving the door out of the way and shuffling into the inside foyer, the lifeless thing heads towards the outside world with just one more push of one more door. It encounters another lock but with another gesture and another clicking sound...the outside world is finally reached.

It staggers from the door, stretching its stiff neck upwards towards the night air. The streetlights outlined its full figure as it struggles to move the torso upwards. It let out a long labored breath and one more time, the bones start to cracking, vertebrae shifts, rib cage lengthens and the shoulder blades spread out. The neck stretches upwards as if to reach for more air, the femurs and knee joints straighten, tendons elongate, cartilages click and the lungs expand. It starts to breathe, taking long breaths in, long breaths out, through the mouth, with no more wheezing. It was tasting air, real air for the first time in days. The skin slowly regained its color and elasticity, covering every inch, coloring every centimeter.

Upon her once wrinkled and shrunken face, now sits a

brilliant smile.

Down the sidewalk leading up to the hospital doors, walks a boy child, very short, with brown skin reflecting in the streetlamps. He took deliberate steps towards the woman that was now stretching her arms. Her chest continued to rise and descend with clear breath. With all the contorting and twisting, the hunched figure now stood as an elderly African American woman with a large pepper colored afro; she shapes and styles it with her hands. Her feet straighten, stabilizing her body in a balanced stance. Her irises open, searching past the dark blue night for light. The little boy walks up to her and stops, looking up at her from his short stature, unfazed by the final contortions of her body. The eyes of the elderly woman look around at the surrounding environment. As the brain adjusts to the information the eyes passes on to it, she looks down at the boy now standing by her side.

"Welcome back! You all better now? I'm very happy to see you. Walk with me...this way." He said, pointing a tiny finger down the street.

FX NOZAKHERE

She felt the tiny hands of this child touch hers and lead her away from the entrance of the hospital. His gentle touch sent waves of sensation through her newly reformed body that she welcomed with another smile. The two walk through the night, an old lady and a little boy in a slow stroll down the sidewalk away from the lights of the hospital at three fourteen in the morning. They soon disappear under the darkness of the trees, into the night.

She looks at the boy closely before asking, "Whose chile you don' occupied? Who you got dere?" The boy looks up at the elderly woman, smiling warmly.

"This child is doing something deeper than sleepwalking. I came upon him looking for you. As you know, we can't let people get wise to what we're doing, so I'm wearing him."

"Oh Lord!" The woman's voice trails off. "You take dis here boy back to his family."

"You need not worry, he is safe...both of him. The him out there and the him that's right here with me now!" The "child" smiles again, but the woman isn't convinced.

"And what if sumting happens? Dat boy gets hurt? You gets hurt?!" Her voice is full of genuine concern.

The boy replies calmly, "Do *not* think I am enjoying this. This boy is sickly, there is something wrong with his breathing…it is very uncomfortable."

"The boy has asthma, a lot of the chil'ren have it." The woman shakes her head, feeling for the child. "Do what you can for him. If you gone take the boys body, the least you could do is fix it up."

The boy looks unaffected by her concerns "It's not my problem right now."

"Psshh!" The elder woman disregards what is said, she looks away to the lit street of Hyde Park as they stroll down the residential area. There is a moment of silence.

"You put that boy back, you hear?" She gently chides him.

The boy smiles and nods his head yes, "I shall."

The elder takes in a clear breath as she looks around with

her newly opened eyes.

"Ah, ev'ry ting looks and feels the same as where I jus come from! Where the others at?" she asks.

The boy pauses for a second, lifting an eyebrow as if in thought. "They"re around, all of them…here somewhere. Some of them messing about, others helping where they can."

"I see. Too many of dem not taking tings serious." She replies.

"But they will…" Was his only response. There was another long moment of silence as they walk until the elder speaks out again. Her voice ringing clear in the night.

"When you travel through like dat, you can see what will be right?" the elder woman asks.

"Yebo," the little boy responds, looking up at the woman.

"And what did you see? Anyting worth coming back to?" Her voice trailing off as if she was asking a question for which she already had the answer.

The boy's smile disappears and he shakes his head slightly.

DuSable City

"Orenda, my sister, I'm afraid something horrible is about to happen in Chicago."

The young boy and the old woman disappear, hand in hand, into the crush of humanity flooding the street on this cold night, lost in the darkness of the underside of Chicago.